LIZZY DUPREE

AND THE THOUSAND-YEAR CRUSH

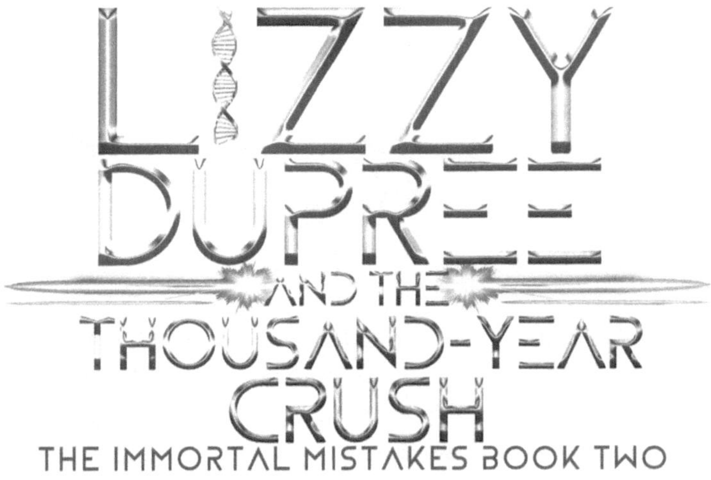

LIZZY DUPREE AND THE THOUSAND-YEAR CRUSH

THE IMMORTAL MISTAKES BOOK TWO

SANDRA L. VASHER

MORTAL
INK PRESS

LIZZY DUPREE AND THE THOUSAND-YEAR CRUSH
Copyright © 2020 by Sandra L. Vasher

ISBN 978-1-950989-04-1

Cover design by Danielle Doolittle | DoElle Designs | www.doelledesigns.wix.com

To all the boys I didn't see. Luckily, I finally woke up and saw the right one, but it was looking kind of rough there for a while.

1.

LIZZY

3442 CE Astronomia Nova

I'm a thousand years into a three-thousand-year space journey when death makes a serious threat to my immortal existence.

I should see it coming, but I don't. I'm on duty on the command deck, and I'm the first person to notice our water levels dropping. I investigate for a minute or so before I find the source of the problem. Then I speak up.

"Water pod eleven is partially disconnected," I tell the others with me. "Water levels dropping."

Commander Rowan, a shrewd woman with admirable girth, immediately turns her attention to the water pod. "Let's get eyes on it," she says, and I pull up a video feed on our central console.

Pod eleven is dangling from the ship.

"Shit," Rowan says under her breath.

Personally, I think that's an underestimate of how bad the situation is. That dangling water pod is a threat to the mission and the entire crew. Our ship, the Astronomia Nova, has twelve water pods, and each is capable of holding an Earth year's worth of water.

Water is *life* for us. It's what we drink, cook, and bathe with. It's what we convert into oxygen when the plant bay isn't pumping out enough. It's what we use to maintain the right gaseous balance in the cerebrospace layer that cushions our biosphere from the many blows the external hull the Astronomia Nova takes.

We recycle as much water as we can, but there's no way to keep it all contained. We lose a few drops every day. If we were only traveling for weeks or months, that might not matter. But we're on a journey scheduled to take millennia, and we're on our own. No one's going to rescue us if we run out of water. We have to keep filling up those pods, or it's game over.

To accomplish that, we typically make pit stops on aster-oids, moons, and small rogue planets that we identify as detectable sources of water. We send drone rovers out with the pods to collect, and we only need to refuel like that once every twelve years or so. But right now we're in a drought. Ten of our pods are empty. It's been that long since we've found a safe place to stop.

Pod eleven was one of the two that were still full. I zoom in with a camera as my colleagues on the command deck gather around the central console. Even though the pod is barely hanging off the ship, we can't see any damage.

One of my colleagues, Myles, points over my shoulder at a place on the screen. He's standing close behind me. I don't think he realizes he does it, but he always stands closer to me than he does to anyone else. And I always know where Myles is standing in relation to me.

"Looks like the leak's coming from there," he says.

I see it, too. There's a tiny fountain of static right where he's pointing. Water must be dribbling out from a leak the cameras can't see. And if the cameras can't see it, the drones won't be able to get to it. We'll have to go out there and fix it ourselves. A spacewalk is required.

"I'll suit up," Myles says, and I don't know why a queasy feeling tingles in my throat.

"Are you sure?" my colleague Yedda says. "It's not your turn. Sterling and I could go. Or Sterling and Xael."

Myles shoots a look at me, and I know what he's thinking. We are a crew of a hundred highly skilled immortal humans. Everyone except our three commanders is eligible for this kind of thing, but it's going to be a risky repair. It needs to be done right, it'll have to be done before we can completely bring the ship to a stop, and we don't entirely know what happened to that pod.

Yedda, Sterling, and Xael are all adequate with emergency repairs, but we need more than adequate out there.

Commander Rowan smacks the side of the console with the back of her palm. "No, we need the right team out there."

"We are *all* qualified," Yedda says, specifically *not* looking at me. I like Yedda, but she's always jumping at the chance to get out into space, especially when she thinks *I* might want to go instead of her. It's silly. I hardly *ever* want to go on a spacewalk. I'm not irrationally afraid or anything. After the first time, there's just nothing fun about a spacewalk. They're cold, dark, and dangerous.

But you don't always get what you want, and what you want doesn't necessarily determine what you should do. So I put an end to the matter. With the truth. "Myles and I are the only team who regularly beats the emergency simulations. I'll suit up, too."

"Go," Commander Rowan says. "We'll get Yedda and Sterling ready on backup."

Myles and I run to the airlock bay, suit up in heavy-duty deep space suits, and wait the least amount of time we possibly can for our suits to pressurize. We release the airlock, and just like that, I'm on a tether attached to a ship in outer space.

We move along the sides of the Astronomia Nova like rock climbers, clipping our tethers to one anchor loop after another and using footholds to push forward. Our suits are equipped with two cables each, and we're using my second to tether to each other. The dual-tether system allows one person at a time to unclip, move forward, then clip back to the ship while the other person remains secured.

Myles and I have done this so many times—in reality and in virtual simulations—that we don't have to talk to coordinate. Even though we're fighting the ship's forward velocity as we make our way from the airlock to the pod, the trek only takes ten minutes. Then we have a closeup view of the pod. There are some tears in the metal where the pod is supposed to be hooked to the ship, and the water leaking out is freezing in sharp icicles that protrude from the pod.

"Think this is from that dust storm we went through a few days ago?" I ask Myles over the radio.

"Hard to say," he says.

In any case, we need to melt that ice and solder patches over the tears, then we can try to reconnect the pod. Myles stays clipped to the main body of the ship and holds the toolkit we brought with us while I clip myself to the pod and do the thawing and soldering. It only makes sense to divide the work this way. It's a delicate job, and I have better dexterity than Myles, especially in a spacesuit.

We're out there for two hours before I'm happy with the

patch repair. All that time, Myles never rushes me. Never tries to backseat solder. Never makes me any less than perfectly confident that I can fix this. He just hands me tools and says things like, "Nice work, Lizzy," and "Looks good," in a calm, even voice.

This is all why we work so well together. We never fight about who should do what. Neither of us is the type to panic. He trusts me to be capable, I trust him to have my back, and vice versa.

I'm about to tell him I'm ready to reconnect the pod when an unexpected interstellar wind yanks the pod away from the ship and me with it.

Interstellar wind. It's not real wind like we used to know on Earth, but our crew astrophysicists haven't decided exactly what it *is* yet. They spend a lot of time arguing about whether the invisible gusts emanate from black holes or maybe clouds of dark matter.

The next time I talk to those nerds, I'm going to tell them the gusts *feel* like violent vacuum suction. I am tethered to Myles and the pod, and after the cable between Myles and me grows taut and threatens to pull him away from the ship, too, I have a split second to choose which cable to unclip.

It's a strange moment for me. Happens slower in my mind than it probably happens in real life. The pod is important. More important than I am to our mission. If I unclip from the pod, we risk losing it permanently. If I unclip from Myles, I might be able to save it.

I unclip from Myles.

It is the best choice, despite that queasy feeling I still have.

I am surprised to hear him yell my name, and I can see his eyes turn red as I am sucked away from the Astronomia Nova with the pod. Red eyes happen to us when we get stressed.

Because we're immortals, and that's one of the side effects of the virus that made us this way. It took me a couple hundred years to decide that Myles's natural eye color is the exact blue of this cozy cashmere sweater I loved back when I was still on Earth. I love those blue eyes of his even more than I loved that sweater. I hate it when they turn red.

I hate it now.

Myles is one of only six humans on our ship who didn't *have* to choose immortality way-back-when to escape an otherwise untimely death or debilitating illness. He is one of the three humans I care most about on the Astronomia Nova. He is one of only two humans on our ship who has never had an intimate relationship with someone else on board.

If you ask him why he'll tell you it's because he's still in love with a girl who broke his heart on Earth. She's the reason he became immortal. She's the reason he refuses to fall in love again. She's the reason he is quick to volunteer for risky spacewalks.

Oh, he can't fool me. Whenever it seems like Myles is acting self-sacrificing and noble, he's really just pursuing a secret death wish he won't admit to having. He doesn't think he has anything to lose since he's already lost *her*. He'd like to make it to the planet Kepler, but only because he's a little curious about what might be there. The tether between Myles and his own life is frayed.

But as for me? Immortality chose me, not the other way around, and I have plenty to lose. There are people I care about, things I want to learn, places I want to see. I *enjoy* life. When I do something that seems self-sacrificing and noble, it's almost always because I'm watching out for the people I love most. Anna, my sister. Maaz, truly my best friend forever.

They're both probably pretty ticked off at me right now.

And Myles.

I can't see Myles's eyes anymore, and that realization shakes me out of a moment of paralysis and tells me that if I ever want to see his blue eyes again, I need to pull it together and get this pod and me back to the ship. After all, regardless of what I just did with that tether, *he* simply isn't something I'm ready to give up on yet. I wasn't done building back the connection he thinks he's lost to humanity. I wasn't done showing him love doesn't need to be so limited.

Myles.

My thousand-year unrequited crush.

I am definitely not ready to give up.

2.

LIZZY

2409 CE Earth

I am twelve years old when my sister Anna gets a black flag on her Standardized Genetic Screening Test. Almost everyone takes the test. It's even offered at schools like the one we attend, where most of the kids are poor, and the classes are overcrowded. It's free, and everyone takes the test because it provides critical information about your future.

Critical like your sister has a black flag.

A death sentence.

Or at least, almost a death sentence. A black flag means Anna is genetically predisposed to a serious illness or condition that is more than 85% likely to kill her before age twenty-seven. For Anna, the serious illness or condition is Concealed Human Immunodeficiency Virus.

CHIV. It's one of the few things the SGST screens for that isn't genetic, but it's still a death sentence. CHIV is a nearly incurable illness that destroys your immune system. It can lie dormant in your body for decades, but once it strikes, your likeliness of being able to survive a mild cold drops like crazy. Rich people with good health insurance get tested for it at their annual physical exams, but poor kids can't afford tests for viruses they shouldn't have.

Without the SGST test, we might not have known Anna has CHIV until she got pneumonia or something and died the same week.

I am crushed and terrified.

Anna is the only family I have that counts. I've met my dad twice. He lives in California with his new family—the one he left us for before I was even born. His one good quality is that he sends large child support checks, and as a little kid, I thought he had a *lucrative* job. As in, mega mob gang boss lucrative. The two times I met him, he seemed to look the part, and he cussed out our mom so bad that I figured he *had* to be living the thug life.

I liked to pretend that he didn't come around more because he was trying to protect us. But Anna told me when I was ten that he's a lawyer, and he has three kids he does care about. Including two other daughters. Daughters he sees every day. And lives with.

In other words, he's a real ass hat. That's something I've heard my uncle call him, usually in the context of "Dupree's an ass hat, Ma, leaving you to take care of those two kids by yourself." Our uncle says the word "kids" like what he really means is "disease-carrying mosquitoes." Anna says this is irony because our uncle can't hold down a job, and lots of times, he lives at his "ma's" house, just like us. He's an ass hat, too.

As for our grandma, she's the one who took us in after our mom died. We don't call her grandma, though. She doesn't like that. She likes us to call her Amaryllis. Her legal name is Mary, but Amaryllis was born in the early 2340s, and she's got the same genetically modified drug addiction that all the hippies of the 2360s seem to have. She thinks she's going to take the Immortality Virus one day and live forever and that Amaryllis is a better "forever name" than something classic like "Mary."

Anna says Amaryllis is going to die of liver disease long before the Immortality Virus becomes available for old people, and I don't think Anna cares if Amaryllis dies. We hardly see any of that child support money our dad sends. Amaryllis spends most of it on drugs and alcohol. But I wish Amaryllis would take care of her liver better. I don't like her much, either, but I don't want her to die of liver disease.

Anyway, I've already watched someone I love die. My mother. It was awful. It took three weeks. By the end, her skin was tissue paper thin, and she had dark purple spots that made it look like someone had taken my markers and dotted her everywhere with them. Her hospital gown was splotched with mucus and streaked with blood. Her body looked like it had caved in on itself.

It was a rare case of measles complicated by pneumonia. That's what Amaryllis told us. But when we get Anna's Standardized Genetic Screening Test back and find out that she's got CHIV, we realize we were lied to.

"She *didn't* just get the measles, Lizzy," Anna says to me as she paces back and forth across our shared bedroom with her SGST results crumpled in her hand. Now that I know Anna has CHIV, I keep looking for signs of her imminent demise. Except for the bright red patches of fury on her face, Anna looks perfectly healthy.

I wonder if maybe her SGST results got mixed up with someone else's. How can Anna possibly have CHIV? Most people who get that disease get it from someone they had sex or shared needles with. Anna is the best person I've ever met. She sets rules for herself, and she never ever breaks them. There's no possible way she's done drugs.

"I don't understand," I say to her. I'm sitting on my bed with my knees pulled up to my chest and my back against the wall. "How can you have CHIV?"

Anna begins to pace a little faster, and those patches of red on her face get bigger. Is she embarrassed? She's fifteen. I don't think she's ever had a boyfriend, but maybe *she's* been lying to me? Maybe she had sex with someone who had CHIV?

"I can't believe no one told us!" Anna says. She's not exactly yelling, but her voice is a lot higher pitched than usual, and the way she is acting makes it harder for me to wrap my mind around everything.

I tuck my knees even closer to my chest and look up at her, hoping she'll tell me the truth if she's ever lied before because this is a critical time for honesty. "Did you … have you …" I am trying to come up with a way to ask my sister, who never sneaks out of the house or comes home late or hangs out with the wrong crowd, if maybe she had sex with someone just once? *Then* it dawns on me that if she's ever had sex, it probably wasn't her choice.

The thought makes me sick. Did someone *rape* Anna? It makes me feel so dizzy to think of someone forcing my sister to have sex with them that I have to put my head between my knees and look down at the bedspread. It is worn and pilly, and threads are coming loose everywhere. I notice some dark wet spots. I'm crying.

I feel Anna's weight sink into the bed next to me, and her arms come around me. "I'm so sorry, Lizzy," she says. "I didn't want this to happen. And I am furious at Mom for—"

I interrupt her because I *need* to know. "I just don't

understand. If someone raped you, why didn't you tell me?"

She *could* have. Told me. I'm younger than Anna, but I've been through a lot. She could have told me. I could have handled it.

She sighs and rubs my back because even though she's the one with the black flag, I'm the one who needs to be comforted. I sniff up my tears and try to pull myself together. But why did this happen to Anna? Why her? Doesn't the universe know I need her?

"I wasn't raped," she says softly, and before I can ask my obvious follow-up question, she adds, "And no, I've never had sex with anyone. I've probably had it since birth. Which means Mom gave it to me. Maybe when she was pregnant or breastfeeding. We were stupid not to realize before. No one dies from measles anymore. No one except people who have CHIV."

"But is that *possible*?" I'm trying to remember anything I've ever learned about CHIV, and all I really know is to be afraid of it. "Can babies get it from their moms?"

Anna grunts. "Probably only if your mom is super irresponsible. I bet rich people have ways to prevent it."

It's not difficult to believe that our mom was super irresponsible, and our family has never been rich, and this truth is both an enormous relief and a terrible betrayal. Suddenly, I'm the one who has bounced up from the bed, and I'm pacing back and forth across the room with my cheeks getting puffed up and red while I think about how our poor-ass mom did something stupid to get CHIV and then did something stupider to pass it right along to Anna and no one could be bothered to tell Anna and me.

I start cussing under my breath, and for once, Anna doesn't bother stopping me. I march around our little room, ranting about how unfair it is that Anna is now paying the price for Mom's actions, how awful it was that no one told us, how infuriating it is that we're in this situation.

"I know," she says. "They should have told us. But … my CHIV could be cured."

There's a cautious tone to her voice that tells me there's even more reason to be furious, but the reason hasn't come out yet. I *do* know Anna can be cured. It's the one potentially bright side to all of this. The Immortality Virus is the only known way to effectively fight CHIV, and Anna happens to be the right age to take the virus. She'll definitely be accepted into the Immortality Program with her black flag. It's just that …

"What if the virus kills you?" I whisper.

She grabs a pillow and smooshes it in her lap aggressively. "That's not very likely."

The Immortality Virus kills two percent of the people who take it, and they only let people who are younger than seventeen take it because it's even more dangerous for adults. So that's two out of a hundred kids who take the Immortality Virus and die. Maybe those odds don't seem bad, but only one out of a thousand kids get a black flag on their SGST reports. I'm not feeling great about Anna's luck today.

"I have a better chance taking it than waiting for CHIV to make me sick," Anna says, sighing again as she stares at me with those dusty gray-green eyes. There's a dark, steel-gray ring around her irises that makes them seem especially entrancing. People tell us our eyes are the same, but they aren't. Hers are deeper than mine, and she can cover up more of what she feels than I can.

She's covering up something now.

I feel my insides begin to shake, even though it's not cold in our room. What else could be wrong here? Is there some reason Anna could be disqualified from the Immortality Program? If she applies, does it mean that she'll never be able to talk to me again? What will happen to me if she dies of the Immortality Virus?

Why is she *looking* at me like that?

"Lizzy, if I have it, you could, too," she says.

Oh. Well, if that's all …

"No, I don't," I tell her, and I am sure that I do not. There's no way. I would know. If something that bad was happening to me, *I would know.*

Anna looks concerned. "Have you been tested?" She screws up her face. "Why would you have been tested for CHIV? Lizzy, you would tell me if—?"

I realize she's now the one wondering if I've done drugs or had sex with someone, and I'm *twelve*, and I have *not*.

I wave my hands frantically. "No! I haven't been tested. I haven't … done anything … I don't need to be tested."

She is glaring at me like I nearly gave her a heart attack. "If you haven't been tested, then how do you know you don't have CHIV?" she demands.

"I just do!" I shout at her. "I don't *feel* like I have it."

Anna lets herself fall onto her side and curls herself around that pillow she's been squeezing so tight. "I don't want you to have to take the Immortality Virus so young, Lizzy." She tucks her face into the pillow. "I don't want either of us to have to do this."

I decide this would be a good time for sisterly cuddling, and I climb back onto the bed with her. "Don't worry," I tell her. I cannot be upset anymore if Anna is upset. Only one of us can cry at a time. "You'll be fine. You won't have any problem with the Immortality Virus. And I don't have CHIV, but when I'm old enough to apply to the Immortality

Program, I will, too, and then I'll become immortal, and you'll never, ever be alone."

She takes my hands and curls close to me. She doesn't say anything else after that, and we both fall to sleep. I am sure I do not need to be tested, but I let Anna drag me to the doctor's office the next day anyway for a test.

I'm positive for CHIV.

3.

LIZZY

Anna and I agree to tell Amaryllis—who never bothered to look at Anna's SGST report herself—at dinner the next day.

"We're going to become immortals," Anna explains to her over fried soy chicken. She says it clearly, matter-of-fact, so that Amaryllis can understand.

But Amaryllis has a glazed look in her eyes. "When?" she asks dreamily.

"We got a message from the Immortality Program today," Anna explains. "We're meeting with the representatives tomorrow. I think we'll have to go live at the Atlanta Immortality Center for a while."

"Immortality," Amaryllis says, dragging the vowels out as if they taste like a sweet drug on her desensitized tongue. "Soon I'll be immortal ..."

But she is asleep the next day when two women come to take us to the Atlanta Immortality Center. They tell us they are both immortal, but we wouldn't have known from their looks. One looks like she's in her late twenties, which means nothing because immortals stop aging after they reach

16

their peak health and spend the rest of their lives looking like they're somewhere around twenty-seven years old. The other appears closer to Anna's age, which probably means she became an immortal more recently, but there are still no tell-tale signs.

They introduce themselves to us like maybe we're more than just two poor little girls trying to escape an unfortunate fate. Then they come inside Amaryllis's tiny house, and it only takes a moment and a glance for the older woman to say to the younger, "Would you tell the driver we want to add a stop at AmazoMart?"

Anna holds up the one duffel bag we packed, which contains all our belongings, and says, "But we have everything we need."

"And we don't have any money," I add before Anna elbows me hard and says, "shh!"

The women are kind to us. We're part of the immortal community now, they say. They tell us we won't need money.

"But we're not immortals yet," Anna says.

"Oh, don't worry about that," the younger woman tells us. "You're both *going* to take the Immortality Virus injection, aren't you? You're with us now. We take care of our own."

We try to say goodbye to Amaryllis, but she's too doped up for us to wake her. We leave a note for her instead, then we ride away with two strange women who proceed to take us on the wildest shopping spree we have ever experienced.

We go to five different stores. The women shower us with brand new shoes and clothes no one else has ever worn. They teach us what it means to "accessorize," and we need other things, too. Mobile coms, games, toys, books, new toothbrushes.

Anna keeps saying, "But what if we don't survive the

Immortality Virus?" and the women laugh off her concerns.

"If you only have weeks left to live, then you are especially worth splurging on," the younger one says, and she hugs Anna. It's so weird. No one ever hugs us except each other.

They settle us into a cozy little dorm room at the Atlanta Immortality Center, show us where the cafeteria is, introduce us to some of the other girls living on the same floor as ours, and tell us they'll be back tomorrow morning to give us a tour of the Immortality Center campus.

Those two strange women treat us better in one day than anyone else in our actual family has ever treated us our whole lives.

"We need to remember this if we survive, Lizzy," Anna whispers to me that night as we're trying to fall to sleep for the first time in a new room.

"I could never forget a day like today," I tell her. I'm practically still floating on the high.

"I meant the way those women treated us," Anna said. "Like we were *all* sisters. It felt good, didn't it?"

I agree with her, but I don't want her to think anyone could ever replace her. "Anna, you're always going to be my best sister," I tell her.

"You're my best sister, too," she says, and we sleep more soundly that night with our black flags hanging over our heads than we ever have.

Sisterhood. We don't know it that day, but it's one of the things Anna and I will be proudest to take with us to Kepler thousands of years from now. Anna says the love between sisters is the purest form of love. It's so much less complicated and dangerous than stupid romantic love.

And I'm still only twelve. So right then, I agree with Anna. I don't know how to make friends with boys right now anyway, much less how to kiss one, and things between my sister and me are still good.

Sister love is the best.

Two weeks after Anna and I arrive at the Atlanta Immortality Center, I take the Immortality Virus injection and become the youngest immortal in the United States.

Immortality suits me from the start. Most people who take the injection get really sick after. Some don't live through it. Me? I only feel like I have a bad flu. For three days, I run a fever, try to cough out my lungs, and sleep a lot. Then it's over, I'm immortal, and I feel great.

Immortality does *not* suit my sister.

Anna and I get our injections together, and at first, we go through the sickness together in the same hospital room. But soon, the nurses tell me Anna is "a little" sicker than I am, and she needs to be taken out of my room so she can have special care. They tell me this is normal. She's older than I am. The older you are when you take the virus, the harder it is for your body to adjust. I play around in the children's ward of the hospital for two weeks, while Anna nearly dies from the injection.

I don't know until later just how bad it got for her. She became violently ill. Her fever lasted a full ten days. Her respiratory inflammation was so bad she coughed up blood. She was dehydrated and delirious, and she coded three times.

You know how in those dystopian novels of the early third millennium, whenever a virus comes into play, it's always as, like, an uncontrollable plague or some nefarious government elimination program? That's not at all what happens with me, Anna, or anyone else who takes the Immortality Virus.

Our hospital is equipped for this. Our doctors and nurses do everything they can to help every single patient survive. Most patients do survive.

Anna survives, but she's never the same again.

I love all the possibilities of immortality. Sometimes, when I think of all the things I could do with all that time, I feel so excited I can barely contain it all.

"We're immortals," I say to Anna sometimes. "We get to live *forever.*"

Anna never feels the same way I feel. She is overwhelmed by immortality. "But Lizzy," she says. "What if we *do* stay immortal forever? What if there's never a way out?"

When she says stuff like that, I think about what it would be like to die. I get a cold, empty feeling in my toes and my neck, like my body is saying it doesn't want to be reminded that one day it could decay. "Why would you want a way out?" I always ask her. I never understand why she can't feel the way I feel about immortality.

Of course, we *will* both die someday. Probably. Eventually. Even as immortals, we're not invincible. Immortality doesn't mean we can't be killed. Immortals aren't stronger, smarter, or prettier than other humans. We can be wounded, we can bleed, we can get food poisoning. But we have such incredible cell regeneration abilities that we hardly age at all past our prime, and we hardly ever get sick. The Immortality Virus is the best cure humans ever invented for cancer, heart disease, dementia. Immortals are always living their best lives.

Mostly. The Immortality Virus used to cause terrible side effects. Anna and I get the newest strain of the virus, IV-1040, but even that version leaves a few unpleasant side effects. Our eyes get itchy and red when we're upset, we have a tendency to act impulsively. But it's all stress-related. If you can control your stress, you can avoid most of the side effects most of the time, so the Immortality Program prioritizes teaching new immortals how to manage stress.

And I hardly experience any side effects at first. Life at the Atlanta Immortality Center is so much better than it ever was before that I feel like I've woken up in a fairytale. Everything we need is provided, and I love the sunny little dorm Anna and I share. Plus, I am so young that I'm everyone's pet. No one treats me poorly. I make plenty of friends.

But Anna has a harder time with the side effects. Her emotions go up in down in huge waves she can't control. She gets migraine headaches, and she is angry, disappointed, frustrated, sad, nervous. I get used to seeing her stomp around our dorm with red eyes, ranting about all the little psychological injuries our childhood inflicted on us.

I try to help. I make soft suggestions about ways she could look on the bright side or at least distract herself from all those negative thoughts. Sometimes she tries, but nothing I suggest ever has the result I'm hoping for. She challenges herself with a heavy college class schedule and ends up using her enhanced vocabulary to talk like a fatalist. She volunteers to work at a women's shelter and internalizes all the pain she sees there. She writes poetry about being born unlucky and dying a hundred years at a time.

It's hard for me to understand. Anna thinks we didn't get a fair shake at life, but I think it's *way* too early to decide that. We're going to live forever. We have *years* to decide what was and wasn't fair in our lives. We have years to change things. And anyway, no one gets a free pass at life, do they? At least we weren't born in an era where having lousy parents would have meant being sold off or cast aside in an orphanage or possibly just being tossed out on the streets. We could have died *long* before Anna was old enough for an existential crisis.

As it is, we're immortals, and our community really does take care of its own. We have everything we need from room and board to solid educational opportunities. We are safer than we've ever been, and we aren't prisoners, either. We are free to come and go from the Immortality Center campus if we want, but we don't have to. The campus is very self-contained. It has a little commercial area with shops, cafes, and even a theater. If we want to leave for some reason, there's usually someone who will drive us. Maybe we aren't as lucky as the kids who can go home to do their laundry on the weekends, but at least Anna and I are alive and together. What else do we need?

Anna is eighteen years old, and I am fourteen when I decide that she isn't just having a little trouble adjusting to immortality. Immortality is suffocating her. And I don't want to blame her for it—or really even admit it out loud—but by then, Anna is failing me.

I have lots of friends to talk to, but none my own age, and the big sister I want is practically removed from my life. I can barely talk to Anna about anything. Our priorities are completely misaligned. I don't want to ruminate on the meaning of life or the ethical implications of immortality. At fourteen, I only ruminate about how to sneak into parties the sixteen- and seventeen-year-old immortals are throwing and whether this guy who studies with Anna is secretly her boyfriend. I think he's hot. She refuses to comment.

I'm bored and lonely, and I start getting in some trouble. I stay up late and don't bother doing homework. My grades slip. I get caught drinking beer with some of the new kids at the Immortality Center, even though I'm still not old enough to join them in the official Immortality Training Program.

And that is when some of the adults watching out for me step in. The older woman who came to get Anna and me from Amaryliss's place sits me down one day and says, "Lizzy, I know you're anxious to begin the training program, but until you're old enough, I'd like you to start going to the hospital after school. We're down a few volunteers."

"For what?" I ask. I'm aware that this is a "correction," but I'm getting the attention I wanted, so it doesn't bother me.

"There are always a few kids who come in for the injection and don't have anyone there for them while they recover," she explains. "We have a special concierge program for those teens. Our concierges are volunteers who make sure no one ever has to recover from the Immortality Virus alone. I think you'll be perfect for the job."

I am an extrovert, and I like people. I can't imagine what it would be like to go through the Immortality Virus injection completely alone. I agree right away to volunteer, and that is how I eventually meet my best friend, Maaz Jyoshi. It is incredibly lucky. Maaz is just like me if I had been born male. He makes it *much* easier for me to get in trouble as a teenager. I'm not sure that's precisely the effect my adult mentors wanted. But I'm happy again.

4.
MAAZ

2413 CE Earth

I am sixteen years old when I meet Lizzy Dupree, and I am in love the minute she steps into my hospital room.

She is carrying a tray with a bowl of hospital soup, a container of yogurt, and a paper cup of tea. It is November, and it has been a cold fall, so she is wearing a pink scrub smock over a black thermal bodysuit. Her hair is tied into a curly ponytail, and she's carrying a satchel over her shoulder. It's open, and she's got the weirdest stuff inside that bag. A hairbrush. A pair of striped socks. Multi-colored smart glasses. Duct tape.

"Hey, you're awake," she says to me as she sets the tray down on a hospital table and swings the table around to me. She is wearing a name tag that says, "L. Dupree."

I'm weak, and I spent the last three days vomiting, coughing, and believing that the Immortality Virus was killing me. There are parts I barely even remember after I was injected because that's how dehydrated and sick I was. I'm *still* sick. I need Ms. Dupree's help sitting up.

She smells like something Hawaiian. Pineapple maybe. Or coconut. Then I catch a whiff of the soup she carried in, and it smells pretty good too. Savory. Like this chicken noodle soup one of my better foster moms cooked for me once. My stomach makes a mortifying rumbling noise.

Ms. Dupree smiles at me, whips a cellophane-packaged set of utensils out from her satchel, and grabs my chart. "Let's see ... Maaz Jyoshi from Smyrna. Looks like this is your fourth day out from the injection. Congratulations. You're not going to die. You're immortal!" She grins, points the chart at herself, and bows. "And I, Lizzy Dupree, am here at your service while you adjust to that amazing reality over the next few days. I'll probably be the first person to see your eyes turn red."

I am taking a slurp of soup. It's not thick like the chicken noodle soup it smelled like. It's brothy and doesn't have much to it. But I haven't been able to keep anything down since the Immortality Virus entered my system, and my stomach welcomes the soup.

"So, how are you feeling?" Lizzy asks.

At this point, my impression is that immortality is a bitch, and I haven't even had time to start experiencing side effects. I was told before I did this that immortals are more sensitive to stress than mortals. They're—*we're*—more likely to experience major mood swings, weird blood pressure drops, high sensitivity to emotion.

And the eyes ... mine already feel a little itchy. If things get intense for me, they'll turn red. The whites of my eyes will become bloodshot while my pupils dilate so big you can barely see my irises. I read before my injection that every time an immortal's eyes turn stressed-the-hell-out-red, the pigment in their eyes breaks down just a little. A few thousand years from now, my eyes might only *ever* look grayish red.

I take another sip of soup while Lizzy watches me. Her eyes are like blue and brown watercolors swirled together. They're the prettiest eyes I've ever seen, and I am sad to think of her eye color fading at all. I could watch her watching me all day.

Which I should *not* do. Because that would be weird.

"Are you a nurse?" I ask her, thinking I need to talk to stop myself from staring just because a pretty girl who I think might be my age is smiling at me.

She sits down on the edge of my bed. "Nah. I'm an immortality concierge. It's a volunteer gig."

I don't remember anyone mentioning anything about "immortality concierges" back at the Immortality Center. I'm a black flag—apparently, my heart was going to give out any day—so I had to go through their expedited program. Maybe that was something they forgot to mention?

"You're wondering why you didn't know about immortality concierges before," Lizzy says, exactly like she can read the question on my face. "There aren't enough volunteers for everyone to get one. You have to be special to be assigned a concierge."

She has a few freckles sprinkled across her face. They're hard to see against her skin, but they're a pop of cute accentuating a small nose, a regal forehead, and a jaw structure that would have kept her from ever acquiring a double-chin, even if she were mortal. But since she's probably immortal, this just means she's going to get prettier and prettier until she reaches prime prettiness. Then she'll stay perfectly pretty for the rest of her life.

I wonder what she sees as she looks at me? Does she think I'll be attractive when I'm in my prime? Does she think I'm attractive now? What kind of "special" is she talking about?

Lizzy is looking at my chart. What's in that thing? Records of how often I've vomited over the last few days? Notes about how many times fluids had to be pushed into me to prevent me from dying of dehydration? Bet all that makes me look *real* attractive. Not that it matters. Mortal or immortal, this girl would always have been out of my league.

I focus on my soup. "Does it say in there what I did to be special enough for a visit from an immortality concierge?"

She sets the chart down and points her nose haughtily into the air. "No, *that* file is classified," she says, and it actually makes me start laughing, which apparently makes her laugh, too, and then we're both laughing over nothing until we hear someone sobbing in the hallway. Someone's family, probably. It must mean one of the other patients who recently took the Immortality Virus didn't survive.

Lizzy looks guiltily at me, gets up, and closes the door to my room. "Sorry about that," she says. "It's horrible when someone doesn't make it."

I nod, thinking about whoever just found out their teenage son or daughter is now dead. Was the kid someone who went through the Immortality Program because they just wanted to be immortal? If so, what a pointless risk. But it's more likely that whoever died had a red flag.

I imagine having a parent alive to worry about you making a decision like immortality based on a red flag. Or some close family member who wouldn't have wanted you shorted out of whatever time you were supposed to have left. Someone who hoped the Immortality Virus would give you more time.

If I'd died, no one would have cared. The immortals who picked me up from the group home I'd been living in seemed nice. The nurse who gave me my injection called me "baby boy" with a deep Southern accent right after she gave me the injection. "Now, baby boy, you just relax and focus on your health. Don't you worry 'bout anything else." But none of those people really knew me. None of them loved me enough that they'd have said anything more than "that's too bad" if they found out I hadn't made it.

Lizzy seems to know what I'm thinking about again. She puts her hand on my forearm. "Maaz, just because you didn't have anyone to worry about you when you were mortal, doesn't mean you won't have someone to worry about you now. No one came to see me or my sister when we went through it either." She waves her hand up and down at her pink scrubs. "That's why I do this now. Because if you have to go down thinking you're all alone, you should at least wake up to find out that someone cares."

Ahh. So that's why I'm special. Immortality concierge is another word for "person designated to pretend to care if you don't have anyone else." This also means she knows about my past. She knows I'm an orphan without any siblings. Knows that I've been bounced around through so many foster and group homes that I never have any friends. Maybe she even knows that I've only finished a school year in the same place I started once and that I've flunked algebra three times because of that. I grab the paper cup of tea and try to hide behind it, averting my eyes away from Lizzy and toward the scuzzy chair she deliberately avoided sitting on.

"Sorry," she says. "If it makes you feel better, they only tell me the basics. I didn't read some long, classified file about you. I don't know how your life sucked before. You don't have to talk about it unless you want, and I won't judge you either way. My life wasn't great before immortality, either."

I look back at her, and I think staring into Lizzy Dupree's

eyes is like a balm for frayed nerves. All the embarrassment washes away, and I suddenly want to tell her things. I want her to be my confidant. I want her to be my friend.

She lets go of my wrist and stands up. She looks concerned, and I realize I probably still look upset. I reach back desperately for her hand and catch it before she can get any further away. Her hand fits exactly right in mine, and a buzz like recognition flickers through me.

"Please don't go," I say. "You're right. I don't have anyone. Foster kid. Dead parents. Sordid history of abuse and neglect."

She doesn't let a single emotion come over her face at any of that except for acknowledgment, but I do see something in her eyes. She understands me. I'm safe with her.

Lizzy squeezes my hand and sits back down on the bed. "I had to go through this when I was twelve. I had a black flag, too. CHIV. I've been kind of a weird case for them because I was so young, but I'm old enough for the training program this year. We'll probably be in the same training class at the Atlanta Immortality Center. We could be friends."

The buzz has become a feeling inside me like warm water trickling through my chest cavity. At the word "friends," it becomes a rush that almost hurts. I don't want to be *friends* with Lizzy Dupree. We're more than that. I can feel it in my bones.

But I don't tell her that. We just met. And I haven't brushed my teeth in days. It's not like we can be kissing right now instead of talking. So friends would be a good place to start, wouldn't it?

I say, "I'd like that," and then I revel in the extra rush I get from her tossing her hair back and settling in at the foot of my bed like she's going to stay with me all afternoon.

"Great. I have a good feeling about you, Maaz Jyoshi," she says with a grin. "I think we're going to be *best* friends."

Lizzy Dupree could get more done with that smile than most world leaders could get done with a hundred thousand drones.

"I have the same feeling about you," I say.

It is the first lie I tell Lizzy Dupree, but it sure as hell won't be the last. I know from the beginning that Lizzy is both the best and worst thing that will ever happen to me. I won't be surprised if my crush on her kills me one day.

5.

MAAZ

3442 CE Astronomia Nova

Fast forward a thousand years or so, and I'm on a spaceship that is transporting the most valuable thing in the known universe from Earth to the planet Kepler.

Mortal lives.

A hundred thousand of them, frozen as embryos and just waiting for their chance to take a crack at life. Our mission is to get those mortal lives to Kepler, birth them from artificial wombs, and raise them until they don't need us, their immortal caretakers, anymore. When enough mortal humans are living on Kepler, we'll sit back like empty nesters and watch the mortals take the reins. Then it will be their job to build a civilization of humans that can coexist with the native Keplerians.

To help the mortal humans along, we're also transporting other mortal things. Dogs, cats, horses, canaries, salmon, mice. The seeds to sow the first Keplerian rose vines, grapevines, pine trees, oak trees, fruit trees, grains, grasses, and herbs. We're Noah's ark, except we have significantly more than two of everything waiting in our cryogenic chambers.

All that organic stuff we're keeping chilled on ice doesn't even compare to what we're bringing on digital memory drives, either. We have every ebook that was available to download in 2423 when we launched from Earth. The entire Wikipedia archive from that year. Movies, television shows, videos, audio files. Blueprints, spreadsheets, charts, and more document files than an immortal human could read in five thousand years.

If our crew all dies off and some intelligent life form finds our ship one day floating through space, they'll have enough information to get a pretty clear idea of what humans were capable of—all the good, bad, beautiful, and downright ugly.

That's where our job is especially tricky. The mortal human Keplerians must be better—a hundred times better, a *million* times better—than any human on Earth ever was. They have to come in peace as an alien species to a planet that already has life and figure out how to get along there.

And we better hope they get it right. Because *our* mission isn't the only one heading to Kepler. This is an interstellar correction from Earth for a major human mistake. Sometime after we land, another ship of humans is going to arrive. But those humans won't be idealistic or ethical. They'll be IV-933 immortals. Rabid humans with no sense of morals. They won't be looking to coexist or collaborate with anyone. They might not even be willing to colonize. As far as we know, all those immortals will want is to dominate their destination planet. They got sent off to Kepler before we knew how flawed IV-933 was or had time to correct it.

They're coming to Kepler. And if we don't endow the mortal humans *we*, a bunch of IV-1040 immortals, put on

Kepler with the right values before the IV-933 immortals show up, then *all* the mortals on Kepler—human and natives—will be in trouble.

That is what I am thinking when I wake up from a sleep shift and learn that there's a leak in one of the ship's water pods. We are carrying precious cargo, we have a critical job to do, and we can't complete that job if we run out of water. The hairs rise on the back of my neck, and I feel that I must get to the command deck and see what's happening.

I find Doctor Foster Hinks there already, arguing with Anna Dupree, and I know why my hackles are up.

"Absolutely not," Foster tells Anna. "You are the *last* person who should be on backup for Lizzy. You know if something goes wrong out there, you won't be able to keep a level head."

"She is my *sister*," Anna says. "If something goes wrong out there, and I'm sitting on my hands in here, I will *never* forgive myself."

Commander Rowan is there with them, looking like she has a migraine.

"I'm sorry, Anna, but the doc is right. If something happens, you're going to have to make me the person you never forgive. You're not replacing Yedda or Sterling on backup." She pats Anna's shoulder. "But relax and don't borrow trouble. It was lucky Lizzy and Myles were both on duty when we spotted the problem. They've aced every emergency simulation we've ever thrown at them."

"And every *real* emergency," Foster reminds us all.

But something is different about this. Any situation

involving Lizzy and Myles Kayes working together makes me paranoid, but they're in trouble this time. I can *feel* it, and I have *excellent* instincts.

"Lizzy and Myles are out there fixing some leak?" I ask, just to confirm.

Anna notices me, and I see the panic in her eyes. Her red eyes. Normally, they're a more stormy hazel like Lizzy's. But the only person Anna Dupree loves on this ship is her sister. If you ask *her* what's the most important thing we're transporting to Kepler, she'll tell you it's Lizzy. *She's* the most valuable resource in the universe in Anna's book.

"Liz volunteered," Foster says with only the slightest tinge of defensiveness. Foster and I mostly get along. It's Myles I have a problem with. But Myles and Foster are tight, and Foster knows I'm not Myles's biggest fan.

"Myles volunteered, and Lizzy agreed that they were the best team to go," Commander Rowan says as if she thinks this will corroborate Foster's story. "But if they hadn't, I'd have *asked* them to do it."

The commander isn't biased for or against anyone, but she clearly doesn't understand all *our* biases. If Myles volunteered first, Lizzy went for him. She'd never let that guy go do something dangerous alone. She's insane about him.

And I *do* mean insane. He is *never* going to fall for her. Something that both offends and placates me.

Foster sticks his foot further in his mouth then. "Knowing Myles, he probably volunteered first because he knew Lizzy was going to have to go."

Anna glares hot poker sticks at Foster. "Lizzy doesn't *need* Myles to protect her."

Foster scoffs at Anna. "I didn't say *that*. Myles knows

he and Lizzy make a good team. He was preempting the inevitable."

I want to punch Foster. I do not want to admit that it has anything to do with the fact that he's right about all of that. Doomed love triangle aside, Lizzy and Myles never screw up. Ever. They *are* the right people to be out there, fixing one of our last two water pods. Still, the sick feeling I have is spreading.

"Request to replace Sterling on backup," I say to Commander Rowan.

"Oh, because *that* makes sense," Foster says sarcastically. "You and Lizzy are the *worst* team on the ship. Have you *ever* successfully completed a crisis simulation?"

That arrogant, self-righteous ass. "At least a dozen times," I tell him. I am bitterly aware that a dozen is a terrible number, though. We run crisis simulations all the time. Lizzy and I have tried *hundreds* together. She always thinks we're going to get better if we practice enough. She has that kind of faith in our friendship.

We never get better.

"Maaz, are you sure you want to go out on backup?" Commander Rowan asks. She says it with more grace than Foster, but she's saying the same thing he was.

I'm sure. I'm *especially* the right person for this, and it has *everything* to do with the fact that Lizzy and I never get better.

I can't explain that to Commander Rowan or Foster, but Anna, at least, understands. I know because her eyes have started to turn hazel again.

"I agree with Maaz," she says. "If I can't be on backup, it has to be him."

Foster throws his hands in the air and turns away from

us, grumbling about how he's still gotta spend thousands of years with fools.

Anna mouths, "thank you," to me, though, and I get impulsive and effusive for a second while I hug her tight and kiss the top of her head. Anna is practically family to me, after all. And she knows I agree with her about something important. The most precious thing on the Astronomia Nova is Anna's sister. Lizzy is the soul of our mission. She is resilience personified. The ultimate unifier. She can befriend anyone, anywhere, anytime. Without her, the mortals we're transporting don't stand a chance.

"If something happens, you have to stay with her as long as you can," I whisper in Anna's ear. "You know that, right? No matter what? You can't, you know, try to remove yourself from her life again. Lizzy needs you."

This is important. Anna has failed Lizzy before. I need to know she won't do it again.

"Just make sure nothing happens to her out there," Anna says.

It's an exchange of promises. Anna has the same bad feeling I have about Lizzy being out there with Myles for a critical repair. Lizzy is brave, and she takes calculated risks other people wouldn't take. Myles is logical, and he lets Lizzy take those risks. After all, Lizzy hardly ever gets it wrong. If she thinks something is worth the risk, it is.

Almost everyone on the crew would tell you that trust is what makes the two of them so impressive in a crisis. Which is all the more reason that I need to be out there with her right now. Me. Not Myles. Not anyone else. Because the only reason Lizzy and I do so *poorly* in emergency simulations is that I'm *not* willing to let her take unnecessary risks.

No, it's not about trust.

I just can't.

And that's why, a few minutes later, I'm shoving by Yedda and Sterling and telling them I don't give a damn if protocol says we don't send out the backup support unless there is an apparent emergency. The bad feeling in the pit of my stomach has turned into full-on nausea. Something is going wrong, or it's about to go wrong, and I can only think about one thing.

Lizzy Dupree.

The unrequited love of my thousand-year life.

6.

LIZZY

3442 CE Astronomia Nova

We have radio contact with each other and with the command deck while we're out here, and as soon as the pod breaks loose, our radio communication with command blows up. Commander Rowan wants a status update, Yedda and Sterling want to know what's going on, and as soon as Myles says, "We just lost Lizzy," the panic rises to a level that makes it impossible for me to hear anything.

I hastily switch off that channel, so all I can hear is the external channel Myles and I are on. He's done the same thing. It's our protocol in a crisis like this. No need for extra confusion. I already have Myles freaking out on me.

"Detach, Liz," he keeps saying. He's not quite shouting, but his voice is tense and meant to persuade, and it gets louder each time he says it. "Let the pod go. We can retrieve it later. You can still get back to the ship."

It's strange. He must think I made the wrong call. When is the last time that happened? Though he is right, to a point. If I want to prioritize saving myself, I should let the pod go and get back to the ship. My spacesuit is equipped with a jet propulsion system, and I could still use that to catch up with the ship if I abandon the pod now. Then we can *probably* use the drone rovers to retrieve the pod later.

But *probably* only happens if the pod doesn't get sucked too far away from the ship. "Not yet," I say to Myles over the radio. "The pod's stuck in this stream of interstellar whatever. I have to get it out before I can abandon it."

"The Astronomia Nova is still *moving*, Lizzy," Myles argues. "Let yourself get too far away, and you won't be able to catch up."

His concern is moot almost as soon as he says it, though. It's taking tons of jet fuel to try to pull the pod out of the wind. About thirty seconds after we start arguing about this, I'm already down so much fuel that I can't make it back to the ship on my own no matter what. But that's okay. This isn't my first rodeo. I'll just wait for a drone rover to rescue me. It's fine. In the meanwhile, I have to rescue the pod.

"Can't lose this water," I tell Myles while I continue to struggle with the pod.

"Damn it, Lizzy!" Myles is shouting. "Are you watching your O2 at all?"

I *hadn't* been, but now I take a quick look. I'm still at seventy-nine percent.

"I have hours of oxygen left," I say cheerfully, though I'm sweating from the effort it's taking to pull this stupid pod out of the interstellar gust, my helmet is getting muggy, and I'm probably using more oxygen than usual from having to exert so much effort.

Myles lets out a string of four-letter words. He peppers that string with my name, and it's almost sweet. He's not the type who swears or cusses, no matter what I do. This time he must think I've done something truly extra. Something that just might kill me if *he* doesn't do something to change the equation.

I tune him out, though, because it's too late for me to catch up with the Astronomia Nova anyway, and I continue to fight the pod until finally, I manage to yank it out of that interstellar wind.

Ha. Lizzy one, freak space wind zero. The pod is mine. And good thing I managed that. The pod has a new tear, and it's leaking water again. But I still have the soldering iron hooked to a loop on my suit. I can fix this while I wait for my rescue.

"Hey Myles, can you ask command to call the rover engineers? I'm going to need a pickup," I say while I go to work on that tear.

He is still cussing.

I don't know why. *I'm* not panicked. Though it is a little eerie out here. There's nothing in sight in any direction anymore, and the only light I can see is the light coming off the headlamp on my helmet. It feels like floating all alone in a vast black void of nothing, which *is* what I'm doing if you think hard about it.

Very strange.

But I still have radio contact, and I'm not the type to panic. There's a reason I'm part of this crew. I don't "freeze" in response to a threat. I don't flee, either. I fight until I win. That's just how I am. I talk into the radio to keep myself from over-thinking it.

"Myles? What's the word on that drone rover?"

He doesn't answer, so he must be talking to command or maybe to the drone rover engineers. The drones are as critical as the pods, so we have a whole team with specialized knowledge about how to program them for new targets, prevent possible collisions, plan for an interstellar anomaly, etcetera, etcetera.

I'm guessing it'll take two or three hours for them to get to me. They'll have to be careful about how they do it. They'll want to figure out why we didn't see that gust coming so that the rescue goes well for the pod and me.

Myles comes back over the radio.

"Lizzy—" His voice sounds unsure and afraid. Two things I've never heard in his voice before. It sets off a flicker of fear that I feel in my toes despite the freezing cold of space.

"Yes?" I draw the word out.

"None of the drones are working right now."

"What?" I didn't hear him right. I couldn't have. What he said makes no sense. The engineers are supposed to maintain the rovers so there's always at least one available if we need it.

Myles sounds grim as he explains further. "It's been a while since we needed to stop. The team decided to overhaul the whole fleet this week. They're trying to get one up and running, but apparently, they're all in pieces. It's … going to take longer than you have."

My brain slows down on that, and I'm silent. I've used up most of my jet fuel, so I'm marooned with six or seven hours of oxygen left. That should have been plenty of time for them to get a drone rover out here.

"Lizzy, you still with me?"

My tongue feels weird. Like it's heavier than normal, though I also have saliva pooling in the back of my throat. I swallow a few times.

"I … don't think I understand."

Myles sighs into the radio. "I don't either," he says. "This isn't supposed to be happening."

He starts rambling after that. Myles doesn't ramble, and it's all incredibly foreign to me. He's saying stuff about how he should have saved me or he should have done something to prevent me from needing to be saved. Maybe if he had been the one soldering or if he'd seen that interstellar wind coming, and other things that make no sense.

He ends on, "This isn't supposed to be happening to *you*, Lizzy. If we had to lose someone again, it should have been *me*."

The word "again." It is especially wrong for this situation. *We've* never lost someone before. If I die today, I'll be the crew's first death. But *Myles* has lost someone before. He lost the girl he loved on Earth. Now he thinks he's about to lose me, and he doesn't want that. Am I that important to him? He's never shown it before—and God knows I've been looking for a sign—but then again, I've never seen perfect, steady, even-keeled Myles lose his cool like this before.

"It's not your fault," I say over the radio to him. I have to repeat it once or twice to make him stop the incessant rambling. "You didn't choose this."

He quiets. Is this why I had that bad feeling earlier? Yesterday, the thought of Myles being heartbroken over me for any reason would have thrilled me. Today, I don't want that at all. I don't want him to hang my death around his neck and wear it for the rest of eternity the same way he wears Stella Dellucci's death.

"It's not the same," I tell him. "We both took this risk. You don't need to feel guilty."

"Lizzy—"

"Stop. They're trying to figure something out, aren't they? I have several hours of oxygen left. Maybe more."

"Yeah. You're right. There's time. They might … figure

something out." He perks up his tone, but I can tell it's artificial. He already has survivor's guilt.

I think about the hundreds of emergency simulations I've participated in. It never goes this bad for me with Myles, but I've had this happen with other partners in simulations. Usually, getting stranded in space for more than six hours means someone dies.

I get a sudden wave of nausea.

I don't know if I'm going to survive this.

Then someone else's voice comes over the radio. A harder voice. A voice much stronger than Myles's more gentle tone.

"Lizzy," the voice says.

It's Maaz, which surprises me since he wasn't on backup. Maybe he figured out I was here and hacked the external line me and Myles are on. It would be just like him to do something like that. Also, my emergency is making me notice things I've never noticed before. Maaz only needs to say my name once to make a new, better feeling warm me up and push the sick back down to my toes.

He's the exact opposite of Myles. He obviously knows I'm in trouble, but he doesn't have to force anything to sound optimistic. He naturally believes in the best possible outcome for the future. Honestly, I'm not sure *I* can drum up that hope right now, but it doesn't matter. Just hearing Maaz say my name makes me less afraid.

"Maaz," I say, returning the greeting with so much relief. "I got myself into trouble again."

"As usual," Maaz says, and it makes me feel *known*, and that helps fight my fear even more.

It's the most precious thing in the universe to have a friend who has stuck with you through your best and worst. Those friends are special. They love you for who you are, who you were, and who you're going to become.

I wonder who Maaz is going to become?

The thought instantly chokes me up.

"Hey Maaz, just in case I don't get back to the ship alive, you know I love you, right?" I say, because you should always make sure to tell your friends you love them. Especially if you are maybe about to die.

"I love you, too, Liz," he says, just like he always does when I tell him I love him. It's easy for me and Maaz to be true with each other about our feelings. I've been telling my best friend I love him for a thousand years, and he's been telling me he loves me for just as long. Neither of us stuffs important emotions into places where no one can see them.

By contrast, I've *never* told Myles I love him. I've kissed him sometimes. Every now and then, I've dragged him into a dark corner to make out with him. Mostly when his mood seems especially bad. It's always casual because he won't allow anything more serious than that. It never leads to sex, even though that kind of thing usually does with anyone else on the crew. Yedda is a fantastic kisser. Sterling has several hidden talents. Foster Hinks is hilarious in bed.

Funny. The two men on the radio with me now are the ones I care most about, and I've never had sex with either of them, and I've only kissed the one I can't say "I love you" to.

I don't think I can even do it now. Though I would really like to say "I love you" to my sister. Actually, if it turns out they can't get me back to the ship, then I want to tell Anna I love her at least a hundred times over the radio before I run out of oxygen. Maybe if I do that, my words will brand themselves on her mind like a recording, and she'll remember them when she needs them. Some people don't need to be reminded that they're loved. Anna isn't one of those people.

"Maaz, is Anna with you by any chance?" I ask. "I'd like to tell her I love her, too."

"She's on the command deck," Myles tells me, and his voice is all broken again. "I can tell them to put her through for you. They can probably put her on a private channel if you want."

"Yeah, let's do that," I say. "Thanks."

"Lizzy, I'm so sorry," Myles whispers.

"Kayes, shut *up*," Maaz says. "She's not dying *today*."

The difference between them is so enormous it makes me laugh. Maaz and Myles rub each other's nerves like sandpaper. I expect that relationship's not going to get better now, but listening to them start bickering feels comfortably familiar. I sort of relax into it. I could listen to Myles being all practical and pessimistic and Maaz being all passionate and persistent for hours. Even if they are fighting.

Then I hear something that makes my fear skyrocket again.

"What are you even *doing* out here?" Myles snaps. "You weren't on backup."

"I had a bad feeling about *you* out here with Lizzy," Maaz snaps back. "So now I'm here, and we're going to get her back to the damned ship."

Oh, f*ck.

My mind whirls around what is happening. Maaz *isn't* talking to us from inside the ship. He didn't hack any channels. He suited up, and now he's outside with Myles, and I *know* what's coming next because I've seen it time after time in our simulations.

Maaz is going to try to save me—he never knows how to let me go—and it's going to get all three of us killed.

7.

LIZZY

2414 CE Earth

Maaz and I are seventeen when we take the Atlanta Immortality Center by storm, and Maaz makes the *best* partner in crime.

Which only means good things at first.

We tear up our classes together. Not in a bad way. Initially, Maaz thinks he's not smart enough for algebra or chemistry. I take this as a self-confidence challenge, and I'm determined to prove him wrong. I make him sign up for classes that are harder than he thinks he can handle, and we study together every day.

When he crushes his first algebra exam in the spring, he's adorably surprised. We're sitting outside in the greenspace by the Immortality Center's education building when the results come in on our mobile coms. Maaz is lying on his back with his long legs stretched out and his arm resting over his eyes, and I'm lying next to him with my knees bent and my toes curled into the grass, but we both sit up right away to look at the results.

I squint at my screen and see that I got a 98%. I'm annoyed that I missed two questions, but it's still a good score. Meanwhile, Maaz stares at his com like the world has come to an end.

"So?" I say.

He hands his com over to me silently. He didn't miss a single problem. Not one.

I hand the com back. "You did awesome!"

"I can't believe I got all those right," he says, and he stares at his com like maybe it's going to change its mind about his exam any minute.

I look around for the shoes I kicked off when we came out here. "Come on," I tell him when I find them. "We're going to celebrate."

"Where?" Maaz says. As if there's nowhere two teenage kids can go in Atlanta to blow off some steam after they ace a difficult exam. I have lots of immortal friends by now, and most of them are older than I am and have access to alcohol. I'm sure it's exactly what we need. Work hard, play hard.

I take Maaz to his first party, where the kids are all doing shots of dirty mortal. I grab two shot glasses and hand one to Maaz.

"What is this?" he asks, looking at the liquor in his shot glass like it's poison.

"Dirty mortal? It's tequila and revitalize serum," I explain. "It's good. The revitalize keeps the alcohol from hitting you too hard."

He is skeptical. "Have you done this before?"

"Sure," I say.

He shrugs and holds up the glass. "Okay, then. To victory over math!"

I hold my glass up, too. "To taking a harder math class in

the summer!"

Maaz laughs, then we both down our dirty mortals, and I learn shortly after that not only is Maaz smarter than he thinks, but he loves to dance, and he'll dance with anyone. He's an instant hit with everyone at the party. We have a blast, we get invited to an after-party, and we end the night howling into a karaoke mic at the Atlanta Immortality Center's late-night recreation hall.

"Is Anna going to be mad that you were out so late?" Maaz says when we finally drag our butts onto a shuttle bus later so Maaz can return to his dorm and I can return to the apartment I share with Anna now.

"Anna spends all her time in her room," I say. "She probably doesn't even know I'm still out."

I'm wrong, though. She *does* know. She screams at me when I get home, and it's far more than the scolding I actually deserve. She screams at me like I remember Amaryllis doing. Her hair is the same kind of a mess, too, and there are the same kind of dark circles under her eyes. I can see the resemblance in their faces.

"What is *wrong* with you?" I scream back. "Are you on drugs or something?"

"I'm *immortal*, Lizzy! And you don't understand *anything*!" Anna screams at the top of her lungs. "That's what's wrong!" Then she turns on me, storms back into her room, and slams the door in my face.

Maaz texts, *is Anna mad?* I'm embarrassed by my sister and ashamed of the fight we just had, so I text back, *she's asleep.*

I don't want to tell him anything, but the next day when I see Maaz in class, he seems to know there's something wrong. He asks me about it at lunch.

"Anna was furious, wasn't she?" he says. "We should have

called and told her where we were going."

"Yeah," I say listlessly. He's right. We should have told Anna. But I don't think she screamed at me because I was out late last night. Secretly, I think she was afraid I'd died, and she was jealous it wasn't her. Sometimes it seems like Anna just wants *out*.

"I'm missing something here, aren't I?" Maaz says. "You're not down today because your sister yelled at you when you got home last night. There's something broken between you two."

It's so accurate, it's profound. The thing about Maaz that I liked best before this moment was how often he laughs. He has an enormous mouth full of bright white teeth, so he's practically the definition of smiling with your teeth. Ever since he learned he could do algebra, there's been a spark in his eyes that makes it seem like he's always waiting for an opportunity to laugh.

Right now, though, there's no spark and no teeth. His mouth is pinched together, and he's looking so deep into my eyes that I feel like maybe he can see something in my soul that even I can't see. He understands me.

And here I thought he was my project.

"Anna was out of control," I admit. "And I don't think she really cares at all when I stay out too late. I think she cares that I enjoy life as an immortal and she doesn't. She's so bitter. It's like she resents me for not being as miserable as her. But what am I supposed to do?"

Maaz takes my hand and folds it between his. "Nothing. It wouldn't matter if you were mortal or immortal. You'd always be better than Anna at feeling good because it's who you are. You have an infinite capacity for joy. It's why everyone likes you so much."

"Everyone except Anna," I say.

"*Even* Anna," he says. "I'm sure of it. She just wishes she could be more like you because being like her sucks. And who knows? Maybe one day you'll rub off on her."

The thought makes me hopeful. I smile at him. "I have years to do it, right?"

He squeezes my hand, and the spark reappears in his eyes. Maaz's eyes look like pools of honey poured over a thorny bronze ring.

"*That's* my Lizzy," he says. "And you have more than years to do it. You have forever."

Maaz is a genuinely beautiful person. If always hoping for the best and never giving up on the people you care about makes him call me "his Lizzy," then I will be his any day of the week. So that is the first time I say it:

"I love you, Maaz."

He laughs, and I think his laughter sounds like warm honey being poured over my *soul*.

"I love you, too, Lizzy."

8.

MAAZ

Lizzy is the whirlwind that sweeps me up into the ocean of life and makes me realize I'm supposed to be there, swimming along with everyone else.

She lives with Anna, who is old enough for one of the apartments with a real kitchen, two bedrooms, and a living room. I have a dorm and a roommate who doesn't like me and does like to get high, so I spend almost as much time at Lizzy and Anna's place as they do.

You'd think I'd get to know Anna as well as I know Lizzy because of this, but I don't. A full year after Lizzy and I start hanging out, I've hardly had a single conversation with Anna. All I know about her is that she looks like a sad, watered-down version of Lizzy, and she spends most of her time studying in her room. She's getting dual degrees in French and philosophy from some university in Paris, so she takes her classes virtually, and that's her excuse for never coming out to say hello.

Lizzy is sunlight personified, but Anna is the cloud in her blue sky, and it worries me. Lizzy starts to say bitter things about her sister.

"That's what you do when you don't feel like making friends," she says about Anna one day when we spot her at the same coffee shop we're at. "You learn how not to look *lonely* sitting at a table drinking coffee by yourself and reading a dusty old book written by a long-dead mortal privileged white man."

"You have read many books written by long-dead mortal privileged white men," I remind her.

"Remind me never to do that again," she says, darkly.

Of course, she's joking. Lizzy hides a big brain behind a sunny disposition, but when she wants to, she can pull out all the stops and learn just about anything she wants. She's got me taking advanced math, chemistry, psychology, history, and literature classes. I think it's one of the ways she avoids boredom.

But when our brains are fried from studying, we think up ways *not* to think. Lizzy says we need to be people who *do things*, and I agree. If she wants to go to a party with some new kids, I'm in. Live comedy show? I'm there for it. Concert for a band we love? Done. Reality adventure experiences we have to talk our way into because we're too poor to actually pay for them? Done and done.

After all, I'm with her on her philosophy of life. Immortality only guarantees the possibility of forever. You never know when your life might end. In the meanwhile, you have to *live,* and for us, that means *not missing anything.*

"Maaz, this is the *only* time in our lives when we're going to be this young," Lizzy announces one night after we're both done reading about Enviro War I and the impact of cool drought warfare on global climate change. "We could have thousands of years to be responsible twenty-somethings. We only get to be teenagers once."

This is how she often starts when she's about to suggest something wild, and I love it. I set down my e-reader and grin. "Yes," I announce back. "We *must* remedy that. We need to go out and *do* something." I lean in toward her. "What should that be?"

Lizzy flashes me that smile that could end wars. "Let's get in *trouble*."

I push my chair back from the table. No hesitation. "Alright, Dupree. I'm in. How exactly are we getting in trouble tonight?"

She practically bounces on the edge of her seat in excitement. "I'm going to call a few people from class and see if anyone wants to do something."

Our "class" is about five hundred other immortal teenagers, and even though we don't know all of them yet, most of them know us. Not sure how that happened, but Lizzy tells me we're the popular kids. That's the only explanation for what occurs next, anyway.

Two hours after Lizzy decides we need to get in trouble, we've smuggled three kegs of beer, at least fifty kids, someone's speaker system, and a bunch of pop-up disco lights into the Immortality Center's swim club. The place is supposed to be closed, and you're not supposed to drink and swim, but we're not worried. Three of our friends are lifeguards who work here, and no one's planning to swim anyway.

Or no one *was* planning to swim until Lizzy's in two or three drinks, and she suggests skinny dipping in the pool.

You tell me *you'd* skip skinny dipping in a pool after dark with a girl you're crazy about and a lot of beer and a gazillion of your pals. No way am I saying no to that. I am the first person to tear off my shorts and jump in.

Lizzy cheers wildly, and I've barely had the chance to shake the water out of my eyes before she strips down to her underwear, prances to the diving board, and splashes in headfirst. We inspire so many people to follow our lead that half the party is mostly naked in the poor a few minutes later, and it's like this crazy teen orgy splash fest.

It is exactly as fun as it sounds, and what I want as this goes on is to find Lizzy in the deep end of the pool and kiss her. Unfortunately, I'm too chicken shit to do something like that. Especially after I see her start making out near the six-foot marker with a guy who sits right behind her in world history. He's not that bright. I am not at all cool with this.

Lizzy has been telling me that half the girls in our class want to date me, but until right this second, I've been ignoring that. Now, there's this roar rushing through my head as I watch her make out with a guy who thinks Barack Obama was one of the popes from the twenty-second century.

I need a distraction, and luckily, one appears right in front of me. Her name is Iris, she's cute, and she's bobbing up and down on her toes because she's almost too short to stand in water that's only four feet deep. I am tall, so four feet of water won't even reach my pecs. I hold my arm out helpfully for Iris to hang onto—wouldn't want to let the poor girl *drown*—and she uses that leverage to push herself up and kiss me.

Very soon after, I am backing Iris and me into the part of the pool that's five feet deep. For privacy. Iris clings to me and giggles when we bump into other kids. Then I do some of the things I'd like to be doing with Lizzy with a girl who is *not* Lizzy, and the next morning, I feel a little hungover and a lot guilty.

I'm not sure why. We're all brand new immortals. The Immortality Center hosts sex education lectures, and they're pretty clear on three basics. One, birth control. It's free at the center's pharmacy and available in many forms. Two, the prerequisites for sex between immortals are consent, mutual respect, and communication. Three, don't hook up with the expectation that a relationship will last forever. It probably won't. Forever is a very long time.

So there's no need for me to have any morning-after remorse about anything Iris and I got up to last night. Iris clearly doesn't. The next day, she texts me a gif of a girly pink fish in a pool, smiling and holding a sign that says, "See you next swim."

I text back a picture of a shark grinning and holding his thumb up. Because I wouldn't mind what happened with Iris last night to happen again. Maybe with some actual privacy this time. But it still wasn't especially satisfying, and I still feel guilt with no discernible origin.

Lizzy figures it out for me, and to my dismay, she does it by summing up her feelings about the guy she spent the party with.

"I don't know, Maaz," she says. "We're all just supposed to be testing the waters and all—" she laughs at her pun "—but something was missing. I didn't want to call him this morning just to talk."

(I'm the one Lizzy called this morning.)

"Iris is adorbs cute, by the way," she adds. "I approve. But you have options if you want them. I can't tell you how many girls asked me if you were my boyfriend last night. And they all want to know if you wear eyeliner! No one believes me when I tell them that dark smudgy line around your eyes is all-natural."

I want to ask Lizzy what *she* thinks of my eyes. I want to tell her that *she* has options. I want to tell her that she doesn't have to invite our whole class if she wants to do something like go skinny dipping at midnight. I'd have made sure she didn't have to do something crazy like that alone!

"I overheard Iris tell someone that your eyes are twenty-four karat gold," Lizzy continues. "She's smitten."

I mute my com and groan so loud my roommate actually notices I'm in our dorm for once and throws his pillow over his head. I believe the term for what is happening to me right now is "friend-zoned."

I ask Iris if she wants to come with Lizzy and me to a movie we wanted to see next weekend, and it turns into a double date. Lizzy moves on to a new guy soon enough, but Iris is sweet and not very complicated, and it's not like I'm looking for someone to fall in love with. She becomes my girlfriend, and having a girlfriend is something that necessarily takes time away from your other friends.

So Lizzy and I don't see each other quite as often after that. We're still best friends. We just drift a little. Don't they say that if you love someone, you should set her free? Well, I let Lizzy fly free and stick to watching her from a safe distance.

What else am I supposed to do?

9.

MAAZ

3442 CE Astronomia Nova

I am nearly to the water pods when it happens. The emergency I knew was coming. I hear Kayes yell Lizzy's name. I come within sight of the pods just in time to see Lizzy blown out into space.

If command goes into a frenzy at that, it's nothing compared to the storm inside me. I turn down the volume on the radio channel to the command deck, and seconds later, I'm tethered to the ship right next to Myles Kayes, who has done *nothing* useful yet to save Lizzy's life.

I prioritize. The first thing to do is tell Lizzy I'm here. I say her name. She hears me, she says my name back and jokes that she's in trouble. Because she's Lizzy Dupree, and in the face of death, Lizzy makes light of the situation and remembers to tell you she loves you.

I tell her I love her, too. I've been doing this for a thousand years, and it stings every single time. I'm not sure she's ever going to understand that when I say "I love you, too," I don't mean, "I love you like an old, reliable friend who's always there for you." I mean, "I love you like my entire life revolves around yours, and there isn't anything I wouldn't give to make you happy and keep you safe."

Then Kayes says *he's* sorry again—because he's a spineless jackwagon who deserves to be swept into outer space—and that sets me off.

"You *should* be sorry," I tell him. "And stop acting like she's going to die out there. She's not."

"The drone rovers are out of commission," he tells me. "The engineer I talked to said they're practically in pieces in the rover bay. She's out of jet fuel. It will be hours before the Nova comes to a complete stop. We don't have cables long enough to reach her. We—"

"Have you ever had to work hard for *anything*, you shit head?" I say. I am so annoyed. Myles Alexander Kayes is nothing but a self-righteous dick. Oh, sure, he has some kind of pathetic love story. Lizzy's told me before. Several times. Usually, after a glass of wine. The story goes like this:

Spoiled, perfect, rich boy crushes hard on pretty, imperfect ghetto girl. Girl has a red flag, so boy decides to become immortal. But, surprise! The girl makes her own decision about what she wants for her life and stays mortal.

Oh, the betrayal! Boy can't take it, and apparently, he doesn't love her enough to stay with her for twenty-five years or whatever time the girl has left as a mortal. He breaks up with her and spends the rest of his immortal life telling people he can't ever love anyone else again. His fragile heart is too shattered.

Bullshit. I don't care *how* betrayed he felt when his girl didn't become immortal. If he actually loved her, he would have sucked it up and stuck it out with her until she died. Those two or three decades would have been a tiny blip at the start of his immortal life. He didn't have to break up with her because she stayed mortal. What kind of d-bag does that?

Answer: the kind the girl *I'm* in love with falls for. I think she likes his hair.

I don't like his *face*.

Also, I don't know how much of that I said out loud—probably not the part about how I'm in love with Lizzy—but I think I said some of it, and I end my rant by yelling, "Why the hell did you let Lizzy *unclip* from *you*?!"

"I never *let* Elizabeth Dupree do *anything*, you entitled, ignorant bastard!" Kayes yells back at me. "I don't make decisions for the people I care about. I only have to *live* with them later. She's the one who decided she needed to try to save the pod!"

"Oh, yeah?" I just about scream. "And who's trying to save *her*?"

Myles Kayes and I don't typically yell at each other—our mutual disdain is normally quieter—but we have never *once* completed a crisis simulation successfully as a team. We do not play well together in the sandbox. In a simulation, we both die, and we get nothing done.

But right this second, with Lizzy's life on the line, I think something about what I just said makes a switch flip for Kayes. As I repeat my question, *"Who's trying to save her?"* I can see the change on his face. He just suddenly looks so taken aback. All his anger and frustration drops away, and it reins in all my anger and frustration for the moment.

He moves our communication to a private channel between him and me—something we probably should have done two minutes ago before we started shouting at each other on a line Lizzy could hear. "*You* are, Maaz," Myles says. "You're the one trying to save her because *you're* the one who loves her. I *know* you don't think I understand, but I do. I know *exactly* what it feels like to be willing to give everything to save someone you love. I know what it feels like to live through a millennium of unrequited love. And I know what it feels like to have to go through that because you failed to save the person you loved. So if you can think of a way to save Lizzy, I will do anything you tell me to do to help. God knows *someone* deserves to be happy on this ship."

Damn it.

My face heats up like it always does when I find out that maybe I was wrong about something. Or someone. I've never heard Myles say something like that out loud. Maybe if he'd said it centuries ago to me, we would have resolved our differences.

Maybe. I still don't like his face.

But I am willing to work with him to save Lizzy, and there's a way we might be able to do it.

"Guys? Are you still there? Did I lose radio communication?" That's her, and she sounds chipper given the situation.

"Still here," I tell her.

"Yeah, we're still here," Myles says, almost at the same time, which makes me cringe, but what are you going to do?

"So, I've been thinking," she says. "Maybe we could all just agree that *no one* needs to come to save me? I'm a big girl. I've lived for a long time. Rather than risk anyone else's life, maybe we could just say goodbye?"

Because she is Lizzy Dupree, she makes that sound like maybe we're on vacation, and she got lost in the city, but no biggie because we can all just meet up at the hotel later.

"Guys? Is that something we could do? Maaz? Myles?"

I roll my eyes, and Myles sees me do it and snickers.

"Don't think that's going to work for us, Liz," he says.

"Definitely not going to work for us," I repeat through gritted teeth. "But here's what we're going to do. Myles is going to disconnect his jetpack and give it to me. Then I'm going to tether up to him, and we'll get me as far out as I can on the cables. I'll unclip, meet you at the pod, and you can use the extra jetpack to get back to the ship."

Myles switches to the private channel between us. "That's going to get you killed."

"Gee, I was hoping it would get *you* killed," I say.

He laughs again. Because we're on laughing terms now?

"More importantly, she's never going to go for it."

"But it's something to try." I try to see what she sees in him. Is it this? This calm, no judgment thing he has going? His stoicism? "And, if it does get me killed—"

I can't say it. I cannot tell Myles Kayes that if I die trying to save Lizzy, I need him to be there for her when I can't be. But I think he sees what I'm trying to say in my face.

"Okay," he says. "It's as good an idea as any. Let's make it happen, Jyoshi."

Lizzy has several protests, which come spewing out with an increasing amount of rage on her end while Myles and I ignore her and execute the first part of my plan. I unhook his jetpack from his suit and get a good grip on it. We both have two tethers—one that we can use to clip to each other and one that we're both using right now to clip to the side of the ship. We rearrange hastily to maximize the length of the tethers, clip one end to the side of the ship, clip the opposite end to me, and clip Myles between the third and fourth tether. Then we kick off from the ship together.

"*No!*" Lizzy is screaming into the radio. "You are *not* leaving Myles without a jetpack. The jetpack is a fundamental safety feature of our spacesuits. You do *not* leave a crew member without a jetpack."

"He'll still be tethered to the ship," I say as we float along far slower than I'd like.

"I'll be fine, Liz," Myles says.

"*This is not okay*," she yells at us, even though she might as well not have a jetpack right now herself. A jetpack with an empty fuel tank is no safety feature worth having.

It's kind of cute how she yells at me and Myles together, though.

"If something happens and he gets disconnected, he'll be an easy rescue," I try to tell her. "Plus, it's not like he'll be out here for long without backup. Yedda and Sterling are probably halfway here already."

Myles switches to the private channel again. "Uh, negative. I've been listening to the command channel on low. Rowan ordered Yedda and Sterling not to come out here. Our astro-whizzes are concerned that we might be in an interstellar wind zone or something."

"And they don't want to risk losing anyone else, huh?"

Myles shrugs. "Three's probably enough for one day."

"Do you even know *how* to think positive?" I ask him.

He tries to scratch his face, and his fingers hit the glass of his helmet. "I … use to," he tells me. "A long time ago."

"Maybe you should try to pick that skill up again," I tell him. "You're a frickin' downer."

"I'll work on it when we're all safe inside the ship again," he says.

We're as far out from the ship as the cables will take him now, so I let him give me a shove, and I start floating away from him.

"You do that, buddy," I say.

"What the hell are you guys *doing*!?" Lizzy sounds totally

exasperated. "Do *not* mute me out again. It is *my* life you are trying to save here. I get a say in what happens to it!"

She'd have been a great mom. "You already got your say," I tell her. "You got it when you decided to risk your life trying to save one of our last two water pods. Congratulations. You saved the pod. Now, your turn is over, and we get to say what happens next."

"Maaz, have I ever told you how much I *hate* you sometimes?" Lizzy says.

I laugh as I get close to reaching the end of the fourth cable, still attaching me to Myles. Then I feel that cable go taut. "Kayes, can you go any farther out?"

"That's the end of the line, Maaz," he says.

"Don't you *dare*, Maaz!" Lizzy says.

"Yep. Well. I still love you, too, Liz," I say, and I have some forward momentum I don't want to waste, so at that, I unclip. My universal locater says Lizzy got pretty far away, and my jetpack is barely going to be enough to get me there.

She knows it.

"But I don't *want* you coming for me!" Lizzy shrieks. "There won't be enough fuel to get *you* back even if you make it to me. Damn it, Maaz! Stay where you are! Do you hear me? *You stay where you are!*"

Myles interrupts. "Hey, Lizzy, how about I get your sister on a channel for you now, huh?"

I've liked him more in the last few minutes than I ever have before. Clever that he's trying to divert her attention while I start using quick bursts of jetpack power to push me forward toward Lizzy. Thank God for those trackers.

"I don't *want* to talk to Anna right now!" Lizzy says. "I want *Maaz* to tell me he isn't risking your life *and* his to save mine!"

"I'm going to get Anna anyway," Myles says. "She's been pretty upset."

"Myles! *Tell* me Maaz isn't off tether right now and that you still have your jetpack!"

"Talking to Anna would be good," I tell Lizzy. "She wanted to come out here herself. I talked her out of it."

"Good! Someone should have talked *you* out of it."

"Probably wouldn't have been possible," Myles says. "Sorry about that, Liz. The man couldn't be stopped."

I let Myles take the brunt of Lizzy's wrath for a couple more minutes over the radio while I slowly approach my target. Then finally, I see the pod and Lizzy hanging off it.

"What were you thinking!?" she screams at me as I approach. "One jetpack won't get us *both* back to the ship!"

What's amazing about Lizzy is that even though she's been face-to-face with her own death for almost an hour by now and even though she's sure someone's going to die, she's dealing with all that stress so well that her eyes *still* haven't turned red. That's phenomenal. *No one* else on the ship can do that. Myles's eyes were bright red back there, and I'm sure mine are now, too. The rage in her gemstone eyes makes her look more beautiful than I've ever seen her before, though.

"This has to be the stupidest thing you have ever done," she says when I get close enough to touch her. Kind of. You can't feel much through our spacesuits.

I hold up Myles's jetpack. "Lose your jetpack and take this one instead," I tell her. "I'm not taking no for an answer. This is how this is going down. Then you are going to unclip from this pod and go back to the ship."

"And leave you here to *die?*"

"And leave me here to babysit the pod," I explain patiently. "I'm still at 96% oxygen. What are you at?" She tries to pull her arm away, so I can't see the monitor on her wrist, but I'm able to grab her arm and pull her close enough to check out the numbers for myself. "You're only at 59%. You can't wait as long as I can. They'll probably have the drones up and running again before I run out."

It's a lie. I'm not sure they'll send anything out for me. Probably not. But it doesn't matter. She thinks my plan is crazy either way. "And what if they *don't?*"

"Then, you can send someone out with another extra jetpack to relieve me until they do."

That sounds reasonable as I'm saying it. It at least doesn't leave me without *any* possibility for survival. Though my chances are a lot slimmer than I want her to believe.

She is glaring the brightest glare at me. "I swear to God, Maaz, if you die out here, I will kill you."

This is one of the last times I'll ever get to see Lizzy Dupree. I always wanted to kiss her, and I wish right now that I hadn't been too afraid to do it, at least once. But that was never what she needed from me, was it? And I knew what I was doing when I came out here. Just like I knew what I was doing when I followed her into space a thousand years ago. I'll never regret it. This girl has had my heart in her hands for as long as I've known her, and honestly, I always thought one day she'd end me by breaking my heart. This is *much* better. Instead, I'll go out with my heart intact and frozen in love with her.

It's lucky if you think about it. After all, the best reason for a heart to stop is because you gave it to someone else, isn't it?

10.

LIZZY

2418 CE Earth

By the time I turn nineteen, Anna has shifted her philosophical moping. Now she's taking theology classes, and she thinks it's the perfect transition because theology is like the study of how humans deal with their own mortality. We were never religious before, but Anna becomes an atheist overnight, and that makes her an even drearier person than she was previously.

Meanwhile, Maaz has another steady girlfriend. Her name is Stephanie, and I don't like her at all, but I can't tell him that because the only reason I have not to like her is that whenever Maaz has a girlfriend, I see him less. He walks Stephanie home, goes to parties with her, studies with her, calls her at night. He doesn't pick up his com right away if I call. He doesn't text back immediately.

I have a new boyfriend every month, but I never find someone I have a real connection to. Anna makes snarky comments about the pointlessness of dating and never has a boyfriend herself. I used to hate how she never wanted to hang out with me anymore, but now I start avoiding Anna myself.

One weekend, Amaryllis comes to visit. She sits at our table and asks for a coke when we offer her tea. She asks a lot of questions about immortality—she seems to think maybe we can give it to her—but when she decides we can't make her immortal, she tells us she's still getting child support checks from our dad. She can't afford to give us any of the money, though, and do we have twenty dollars? Because she had to pay for parking in the visitor lot.

Anna is so angry when Amaryllis leaves that she throws the glass Amaryllis was drinking from at the floor. It smashes everywhere, and when Anna tries to start cleaning things up, she cuts herself on glass and starts to bleed and weep at the same time.

I'm annoyed, but I try to say things to make her feel better. "She doesn't matter anymore," I tell Anna. "We don't need money. We don't have to let her visit again."

Anna looks at me like I'm the most naïve person she knows. "I'm *never* going to forgive her, Lizzy. Not even after she dies. And I don't know how you already have."

I didn't know I had forgiven Amaryllis, but as soon as Anna says it, I believe she's right, and it feels like a terrible, unfair accusation.

"Why are you so mean to me?" I say to Anna, but she just looks disgusted and shuts herself up in her room again, and I'm left feeling more broken than all the glass I need to pick up now.

I text Maaz, and he must get the text right away because when he shows up ten minutes later, the glass is still all over the floor, and so am I, and I am sobbing.

He hugs me exactly the way I need to be hugged. He lets me cry into his shirt until I can't cry anymore. He says all the right things, then he forces me to drink a glass of ice water before we clean up the kitchen together. We order pizza and curl up on the couch under separate blankets and talk for hours.

Somewhere close to midnight, I want to kiss him.

It's confusing. I've never been attracted to Maaz before. He's not my type. He's lean and lanky, where I'm more average curvy. His hands are long, and I have a hard time imagining them on me in any sort of romantic way. He's fit, but I don't think he has the gene you need to build bulky muscles or six-pack abs, and he *does* have the gene for hair on the back of his knuckles, and he has a whole beard thing going on that has never done it for me.

And yet, here he is, sitting with me and talking with me about anything and everything, and he has eyes that seriously belong on a fashion model, and those eyes are sending out sparks that are touching me in ways I've never felt with anyone before, and I want to kiss him.

He stops talking for a second, and there's an expectant buzz in the room that I associate with romance.

"How's Stephanie?" I ask nervously, even though I've never been nervous with Maaz before.

He raises one long eyebrow—does he tweeze those?— and says, "Stephanie and I broke up."

Ahh. Something inside me squeezes my heart tight.

"And, uh, what about—?"

He can't seem to remember my last boyfriend's name. Which is fair because I was only with that guy for a few weeks. Travis and I broke up three days ago. I have a lousy track record with boyfriends. The only guy I know who truly loves me *is* Maaz.

I realize I could never *not* love Maaz. But I love him in a pure, unconditional way, and it is separate from this strange moment of attraction. Nothing would ruin our relationship faster than for me to kiss Maaz now and decide after that I don't really like kissing him. It can't happen. If it happens, I'll lose him forever, and maybe it's because I've never seen romance go right, or maybe it's because my sister is such a train wreck, but I come to the only reasonable conclusion I can.

Maaz is the only person I can truly count on. We can never, ever date.

"Oh, yeah," I lie. "We're still together. Travis is great."

The moment disappears. Maaz leaves shortly after that.

Nothing seems to go right for me for a while.

Maaz is busy.

Anna and I never talk.

I date more guys, but no one is reliable.

Amaryllis dies. Liver disease.

I try to reach out to my dad, and in response, he sends one large check to Anna and me but never calls back. We use it to get a car-share membership, and a complete stranger teaches me how to drive on the skyways.

It all takes a toll on me. I break up with guys faster. I drink more at parties. I start driving myself to parties I want to go to when I don't have a boyfriend and Maaz isn't available. Sometimes I drive myself home.

One night, I leave a party alone, drunk, get behind the wheel of the car, and run a red light trying to get onto the skyway. I get pulled over, and the cop gives me a minor-class DUI. Anna has to bail me out. She's so pissed she doesn't even bother screaming at me for it. I can't bring myself to tell Maaz it happened. I'm too humiliated. And when is he around for me to make a confession like that anyway?

Nothing gets better, and I start to wonder what the point is. Why am I even trying? When no one is ever there for me? When I have a million friends, and I'm still so lonely? So it happens again. I drive myself to a party. I drink. I try to drive myself home. I'm self-destructing. I don't even care when I get pulled over after someone reports that I'm swerving through lanes.

Anna bails me out again, and she's furious, but when we fight about it, all these things pour out of my mouth about how she's a terrible sister, and she might as well have deserted me, and let's just say that when it happens a *third* time, she's angry enough she doesn't bother to bail me out.

In fairness, though, the bail that time is pretty high, and maybe she thinks I need to learn a lesson. I should. Three minor-class DUIs get your license taken away *and* get you fined, and I *still* manage to do it again.

The fourth time, though, instead of running a red light or weaving into the wrong lane, I get onto the skyway and speed into one of the safety barriers. A real accident. Airbags go off, I break my wrist, sirens start blaring.

No one else gets hurt, but that's not the point. This is the kind of thing that gets you more than a fine and community service. If I weren't an immortal, I'd be sent to detox and then to prison for a year. The Immortality Program takes stuff like this *far* more seriously, though, because they view the recklessness it takes for a teenage girl to get four DUIs in six months as a sign that she's experiencing "adverse side effects" from the Immortality Virus.

The same woman who picked me up years ago from Amaryliss's house and later hooked me up with my volunteer job at the hospital picks me up from county jail and takes me directly to a lock-down house for troubled teenage immortals. I get a look at my face in the side mirror as we're driving. I've never seen my eyes look redder.

I am confined to the lock-down house for three years. It's the best and worst thing that ever happens to me. For three years, I follow a strict exercise, diet, and sleep program designed to ensure that my body is as physically balanced as possible. I meditate every morning for an hour, and every evening I engage in some form of intuitive art. My weekends are entirely focused on community service. Everything is about stress management. I learn dozens of ways to breathe deep, reduce my blood pressure and my heart rate, and stop a stress-reaction in its tracks.

Since I can only leave the house with a chaperon and a metal cuff, I have a lot of time on my hands. I take enough college classes to have earned my first degree by the end of my sentence, and that turns out to be another benefit of the lock-down. I get my degree in psychology.

Family can visit any time, but at first, Anna never does, and for weeks after my arrest, she won't return any of my calls or texts. During that time, I'm angrier than I've ever been. I blame her for everything I ever did. Then Anna tries to kill herself and lands in a lock-down house of her own, and I realize she's as messed up as I am. While I've been lashing out at the world, she's been lashing in on herself, and we're both wrecked.

We reconcile. Our wardens think it's crucial for us to redevelop a healthy relationship, and they facilitate supervised visits until we are both well enough not to need the supervision.

As for Maaz? He visits me for the first time three months after I get put in lock-down. That's the first time I'm allowed to have friends visit.

He walks into the house looking like he's expecting metal bars and orange jumpsuits, but actually, the lock-down house is beautiful. Very simplistic. Clean. Nice furniture. Lots of light. Designed to induce calm. And I'm at the lowest point of my life, but I've had three months to get sober and come to terms with all this. I'm grateful for the visit, even if I'm scared to death that Maaz and I might not be okay. Maybe he won't want to be friends with me anymore because of this.

"Thanks for coming, Maaz," I say with an anxious smile as his eyes take everything in. "I'll show you around."

I'm expecting questions, accusations, bitter remarks. But the next thing I know, I'm engulfed in his arms, and the first thing he says is, "I am *so* sorry I wasn't there for you, Lizzy."

"It wasn't your fault," I tell him. "I can take responsibility for my own actions."

He looks straight into my eyes, and I have that feeling I get with him sometimes that he can see every truth inside me.

"It wasn't," I repeat. "And this is probably the best thing that could have happened to me."

I think he partially believes that. He hugs me again, I feel him kiss my head a few times, and I appreciate the affection for what it is. "I'm just glad you didn't get hurt," he says. "I've missed you like crazy. I don't know what I'd do without you."

"I've missed you, too," I tell him. "So much."

11.
MAAZ

Here are the things that Lizzy will tell you about the darkest period of her life:

That what led her there was her own irresponsibility. That she drank too much and didn't respect anyone she dated. That she failed to recognize her sister's clinical depression. That she was stupid-lucky not to end up dead or worse, killing someone else. That as a result, she landed herself in a glorified juvenile detention center for three years, and she is thankful every day for that because it made her a better, stronger person.

Here are the things she will *not* tell you:

That she missed Anna so bad that the only time she tried to make a run from that lock-down house was the night Anna tried to kill herself. Lizzy had a bad feeling, and she was desperate to get to her sister.

That both Dupree girls were prone to alcohol abuse. Anna just preferred to drink alone.

That thanks to Lizzy's accident and Anna's self-harm, both girls took a hundred-year vow of alcohol abstinence.

They both have a tattoo on the inside of their right forearms that reads, "sober is stronger."

That when Anna and Lizzy started talking to each other again, they didn't just chat about nothing. They made *plans.* They got permission from the Immortality Program to organize a non-profit organization for young immortal women at risk of substance abuse. Every Friday night, they held a gathering for young immortal women looking for a safe place to relax, and the sisters facilitated activities like guided meditations and yoga for recovering alcoholics.

That Lizzy learned she was exceptionally skilled at textile arts, and Anna turned out to have culinary arts skills, and both girls entered prestigious competitions with their art hobbies and won impressive awards.

That the Dupree sisters emerged a few years later so much better together than they ever were before that Project Dispatch later recruited them for the space mission to Kepler. Lizzy and Anna are considered "critical" crew members, and not just because Lizzy can fix your pants and Anna can bake lemon bars in space. They both have doctorate degrees in psychology.

Lizzy specializes in positive psychology and stress management, and she is a top-notch therapist. Anna specializes in mania and mood disorders. She has written several papers about the ability of the brain to rewire itself.

They both know everything there is to know about substance abuse.

And as for me? I broke up with the girl I'd been dating when Lizzy got in her accident and made it my job to be involved in the lives of the Dupree sisters. When Lizzy and Anna came out of lock-down, the three of us rented a house together. I got to know Anna for real. I learned how to make her *almost* laugh. I stopped looking for someone to replace Lizzy. Oh, sure, I still went on dates from time-to-time, and I had sex with other women. But it was never more than casual. A man cannot have two masters, and my highest priority from that time forward was to make sure that Lizzy would *always* have someone she could call in an emergency.

As a side note, I was recruited for Project Dispatch with the girls. After all, the Dupree sisters weren't the only ones with time on their hands and a cause during that lock-down period. My areas of expertise? Neuroscience and psychiatry with a particular focus on the areas of the brain responsible for intuition and the sixth sense.

It's real. The sixth sense. Some humans have a more sophisticated sense of it than others, and there are four genes that can make you more or less likely to have it. I have all of them. Which is how I explain my own intuition. I knew Lizzy was in trouble the night she got in that car accident. I had a feeling. I just ignored it. And that was the last time I would ever ignore a feeling like that.

I *always* know when Lizzy needs me. I always know when she's in trouble. Hell, I knew *Myles* was going to be trouble for her the minute we meet him. I just had a bad feeling about him. Right from the start. Right from the moment she fell for him and he rejected her.

It was incredibly insulting, you know. I'd always known Lizzy might fall in love for real one day with someone who wasn't me. Always thought I'd hate the guy for loving her back. Never occurred to me that I might hate him for rejecting her. No one should reject Lizzy. Not even a guy who's sworn off love for good. Lizzy is sunshine when the whole rest of the world is dark. She's the thing that never gives up. The person who always has another hug, another kind word.

And Lizzy would have been good for Myles if he'd let her in. Even I could see that. She knew how to make him smile from the get-go.

It would have been so much easier to hate Myles because I was jealous of him. But I love Lizzy too much to want to see her hurt, so I never did try to get in the way of that. I never forgave him for not falling for her, though, and my bad feeling about him never went away.

12.

LIZZY

2421 CE Earth

I am twenty-four years old when I meet Myles Alexander Kayes. It's our first official day of crew training for the Astronomia Nova. Myles is one of the hundred immortal crew members I'm going to live with for a thousand years on a ship from Earth to a planet called Kepler.

The crew was selected based on a million tests. Physical tests, personality tests, skills tests. The Academy for Global Space Administration (AGSA) chooses every person for a specific combination of those factors. Some of us know each other already. Some of us do not. We have five years to train together—and for the Academy to adjust crews that aren't meshing—before we launch.

I set my eyes on Myles for the first time at orientation. He is in line to pick up breakfast before the "welcome to your new community!" speech they have planned for us. He's standing next to a guy with a friendly face and a head of crazy, springy curls, but Myles himself looks like he's forgotten how to smile.

He's handsome, which is not a word I have ever applied to any of the guys I've been into before. I don't know why. I guess I just always thought it was a silly word, but Myles makes it work for me. He has perfectly mussed tawny hair. A square jaw, zero scruff, and a nose that wouldn't get in the way if you wanted to kiss him. The kind of build that implies he has the right gene for six-pack abs. Sky blue eyes that make him look desperately, romantically sad.

I swear my heart dips and sputters, my skin tingles, and my brain zeros in on that guy the moment I see him. "Sad eyes at ten o'clock," I whisper to Maaz and Anna, who are both with me in the breakfast line. Anna has never indulged any of my crushes because she's an anti-romantic who never meets anyone she thinks is worth dating. She only rolls her eyes while I point out Sad Eyes.

Maaz frowns. "I feel like I should recognize that guy."

"What do you think his name is?" I say.

"Who cares? He looks boring as sin," Anna says behind me. This means she thinks he is unlikely to write poetry or appreciate art. "His name's probably John or Michael or Rob."

I'm going to be very disappointed if his name is John, Michael or Rob. A mystery guy with brooding eyes like that should have an interesting name.

"I feel like we should *already* know his name," Maaz says again. "Is he an actor or something?"

Maaz has a Ph.D. in the study of intuition, and I have learned because of him that intuition isn't something to ignore. Of course, he's right about Sad Eyes, but we don't find out until we all formally introduce ourselves later in a huge group intro session.

The guy is Myles Alexander Kayes. *The* Myles Alexander Kayes. Immortal heir to the Kayes fortune. When we find that out, Maaz mutters, "who leaves behind a fortune for a dicey space exploration trip? None of that money will matter after launch."

"I hope he's thought about leaving it to someone," Anna whispers. "Imagine what that money could do for a non-profit organization."

Maaz snorts. "Does *that* guy look like the type who puts all his money into a non-profit organization?"

Yes, I think. He looks *exactly* like the type who gives away all his money because he looks exactly like the type who doesn't *care* about money. And I don't care about his money or his name either. I care about those eyes. I'm wondering what it would take to light them up.

We spend the rest of the week being put through simulated space crises, which we mostly perform in small, two-person teams. It's a pre-test and a mixer rolled into one. The point is to introduce us to each other and the kinds of emergencies we might have to face together. I don't fail any of my emergencies, no matter who I'm partnered with, but I'm frustrated because both Anna and Maaz get partnered with Myles before I do.

By the time my turn with Myles comes, I feel that the cards are stacked against me. I don't know what my sister or my best friend said to him, but I know *someone* said something suspect because the first thing he says to me is, "Elizabeth Dupree. You're Anna's sister, right? And Jyoshi's friend?"

Myles and I are both suited up already. Our very first test simulation is an emergency repair in an anti-gravity chamber. We are talking through the radio in our headsets.

"Lizzy," I say, and my voice feels weird, but I think that's because of the radio. I hope it's because of the radio. Guys I'm attracted to don't typically make me nervous. "People call me Lizzy."

"Okay, Lizzy. Looks like this is going to require some specialized skills," he says after that. "I'm decent, but your file says dexterity is one of your things."

"Yes," I say.

"Then, you're the lead."

I'm flattered but a little dismayed at his "all business" attitude. Still, I suck it up and get to work, trying to impress him with my skills. He makes a good assistant. He hands me stuff. Holds stuff. Doesn't second guess me, even during that very first time. He does exactly what I tell him to do to get the repair done. It takes us maybe five minutes, then we head out of the anti-gravity chamber, where a stunned trainer tells us that he's *never* seen anyone complete that particular exercise so quickly.

"It was all her," Myles says, pointing to me.

I blush. "It was a team effort." It *was*. When you both have the skills necessary to do something like that, the biggest obstacle to completion is arguing over who does what. Myles and I never argued.

He lifts an eyebrow at my comment, though, and the corner of his mouth also lifts just slightly. We have half an hour of free time before our next assignments, so I suggest a coffee break.

Myles shrugs and comes with me to get coffee.

"So, are you here with anyone?" I ask him over coffee.

"Applied with Foster Hinks," he says. "We're friends. But I think you and your sister are the only people on the crew with family."

"Maaz is my family, too," I point out. "We've been best

friends since we were kids."

"Hmm." Myles sips his coffee.

"What?" I ask him, thinking that his eyes might be more like light-wash denim blue than sky blue.

But I can't read his face as he responds with, "It's nice to have family that cares about you so much."

It makes me suspicious. "What did Maaz say to you?"

"Nothing," he says.

"*What?*"

"Nothing important."

"Did Anna say something?"

"No."

I frown at him. "Emotional aptitude is one of my strengths. Did you read *that* in my file? I know one of them said something weird."

Myles almost smiles at me. "Fine. *Diplomacy* is one of mine. But if you have to know, your sister told me to leave you alone. Something about you two not believing in love because love didn't work for your parents?"

I gasp. "She didn't!"

Now he actually *does* smile. "The exact quote was 'We've sworn off love for good, because it ruined our parents.' You'll have to tell me the story on that someday."

Omg. That was Anna being morose as usual. There was no special story behind that! She just says horrible things sometimes when she's thinking horrible things about life.

"It is *far* too early in our immortal lives to swear off love!" I say. And Anna is in *trouble*. "What did Maaz say?"

Myles's face becomes *playfully* straight. "Exactly what you said. That you've known each other for years." Then he adds slyly. "And he may have said something about if anyone ever hurt you, they'd have to answer to him."

So Maaz threatened Myles. That, at least, was cute. Maaz acting like he's my brother or something.

"Well, I guess *he* isn't in trouble."

Myles laughs, and I'm done for. I could stare at his face for hours. I can't believe Anna told him I'd sworn off love! How did that seem like a good idea to her?

Myles and I exchange stories about our backgrounds for the next few minutes. I learn that he and Foster have been friends practically their entire lives, that he had to leave his home and apply for emancipation to become an immortal, and that "there was a girl." She's mortal, though, and they broke up, so the girl isn't something I'm worried about. Yet.

He learns that my mom is dead, my dad is a jerk, they had an affair, and I love my sister more than anyone else in the world. I tell him I'm starting to worry about how Maaz never dates anyone seriously, but I've never met anyone who truly lives up to Maaz. If Myles knows any super pretty, super smart, super nice girls, I could use some help setting up my best friend.

Myles seems particularly amused at that. "You don't think he's ever met any super pretty, super smart, super nice girls?" he says.

The more we talk, the more Myles smiles, until his eyes almost don't look sad anymore. We lose track of time, and when we realize we're going to be late to our next exercises, we stand up laughing and feeling equally embarrassed, I'm sure.

Then I do something rash that I will later blame on the Immortality Virus.

I kiss him.

I just do it. I lean up and put my hands on his shoulders and wait one second for his eyes to sort of recognize what's happening. I give him one more second to back away if he wants, and when he doesn't, I kiss him.

He kisses back, and it is so damn good, but it's only a few seconds before he pulls away with a surprised look on his face. I suspect immediately that the surprise has more to do with him kissing back than me kissing him to begin with.

"I ... can't," he says, and he gets adorably flustered as he continues on. "I don't want to ... I mean ... I *would* like to kiss you, but ... I'm still in love with the other girl. Lizzy, you have to understand, I would never want to hurt someone the way *she* hurt me."

Ahh. I get it. He *is* attracted to me. I *knew* there was something there. But his heart is still broken over this girl. Okay. Fine. My heart makes a decision that my brain agrees is a good one. I have forever with Myles. The girl who broke his heart will be long gone when forever for *us* has still barely started. If his heart needs time to heal, I can give him time.

And I happen to have practice with casual relationships. It's all I've ever done with boys so far. So I smile and flip my hair back with a flick of my wrist.

"But that wasn't love, Myles," I tell him. "That was distraction."

"Ahh," he says. "Distraction." Then he smiles again. "Well, it was a good distraction."

I think so too, and I settle in for a wait.

It will be an impossibly long wait.

13.
MYLES

3442 CE Astronomia Nova

Elizabeth Dupree is the second most stubborn person I've ever met. Stella Rose Dellucci was, of course, the first. But Stella's stubbornness was a different flavor from Lizzy's. Stella was sensitive, thoughtful, delicate. She was the kind of girl who could have carried the world's most fragile secret in the palm of her hand for a mile without breaking it, and yet, she let whatever love she had for me break her.

I would give anything to have a do-over with Stella. Play things out again. Make different choices. Listen better. Be the person she really needed instead of what I thought she needed. Grow old with her. Die in her arms.

Instead, I've had a thousand years with Lizzy Dupree, a woman who is, in so many ways, Stella's opposite. Lizzy is resilient, impulsive, fearless. When she laughs, she laughs with her entire self. When she cries, she cries until she passes out. When she wants something, she goes after it relentlessly. She usually gets what she wants.

I've never been able to imagine Stella's eyes turning red.

I can imagine it on Lizzy, but in a thousand years, I've never actually seen Lizzy's eyes turn red. She's the only immortal on the ship capable of managing her own stress well enough for that. My buddy Foster says it's because she allows herself to feel things. "Human emotions evolved as signals that tell us what we need at any given time to avoid distress. Lizzy is exceptional at recognizing her emotions and giving herself what she needs based on what she feels."

Foster is one of our doctors. He needs a scientific explanation for everything. The rest of us just marvel at Lizzy's talent. And she has more than emotional talent. Lizzy is good at just about everything she attempts.

She is particularly good at fixing broken things. Lizzy can patch fabric, sew up a wound with perfect stitches, put defunct mechanical devices back together, heal a rift between two crew members. She just has a knack for that stuff. Hell, she's been trying to fix me since she met me.

Honestly, I bet it's one of the only things she's ever wanted and not gotten, and I'm not counting her out yet. Lizzy has this glow that radiates around her and infuses everything with goodness, and I'd be lying if I said I wasn't attracted to her. *Everyone* is attracted to her. Who isn't attracted to sunlight?

She kisses everyone. Most people on this ship do. But when she kisses me, I always feel like we've entered a special danger zone. I suppose I like to flatter myself thinking that if I ever fell in love with Lizzy, I'd be so much further gone than anyone else ever could be that I'd never let her out of my sight. My track record with love is nothing short of all-consuming, after all, and Lizzy is worthy of an all-consuming love.

I think if I fell for her, it would ruin us both. I wouldn't know who I was anymore, and Lizzy? Well, Lizzy needs *freedom*. The epic love of her life needs to be someone who would never take that away from her. Who would never try to pin her down for fear of losing her.

Anyway, maybe I can't fall in love. With her or anyone. My heart was sold off, lock, stock, and barrel, so long ago, I sometimes can't feel it beating anymore. Lizzy deserves someone with a beating heart. She should find someone better. She should love someone better. Someone who loves her in the all-consuming, eternity kind of way she deserves.

He's already waiting for her, too. Someone better. Maaz Jyoshi has been giving Lizzy the freedom she needs to roam for a thousand years, and in the meanwhile, he's been exactly what she always needs. Her best friend. Her protector. Her rock. The person who's there when no one else is.

Maaz is a million times better for Lizzy than I ever could be, and as I watch him float off to save her, I am sickened at the thought that Lizzy is about to find out Maaz loves her *far* more than she realized. Then she's going to lose him forever, and the person she'll be stuck with instead is *me*.

"Myles! What the hell is happening out there?"

That's Anna Dupree talking from the command deck. Anna has a special place in my dead heart because she's deader than I am, and no one knows why. The only person she loves is Lizzy, and she's probably panicked about what's happening right now because it's not like we've been updating command very well, have we? Until a minute or so ago, we were busy focusing on saving Lizzy.

I'm 99% sure Maaz has managed that.

"Don't worry," I tell Anna—and anyone else listening. "Maaz went after her."

I can hear Anna sigh in relief. So apparently *she* knew about Maaz's thing for Lizzy. Huh. How about that?

"Then she's okay," Anna says.

"Yes, but *he* might not be," I say.

"Maaz knows what he's doing," Anna says firmly.

"Can we send someone else out for him?" I say. "We are going after the water pod, right? When the drone rovers are fixed? We could send someone to take his place in a few hours like he's doing for Lizzy now. Trade in and out until we have a rover ready?"

There's no noise for a minute, and that's bad, but not unexpected.

Commander Rowan is the next person to speak. "Maaz would be a regrettable lose," she says carefully. "But we can't afford to risk anyone else's life out there. We don't know enough about what caused that interstellar wind in the first place."

There's no use arguing. I know Commander Rowan at this point. Her decision isn't going to change. So I take a moment of silence, and I do something I haven't done in many many eons. I send a prayer out into the universe. For Maaz. If there's a way to bring him back in, we'd all appreciate for some higher power to make that happen.

Anna breaks the silence.

"Myles, you can't tell Lizzy until she's back inside the ship. If you tell her, she won't come in, and then we might lose them both."

I'm not sure the higher power heard me.

"Myles? *Promise* me," Anna says.

"What makes you think I can force Lizzy inside?" I say, but I think I understand even before Anna says it over the radio.

"Because Lizzy would do anything for you, stupid!"

Thank *God* Lizzy didn't hear that.

"Myles? *Promise.*"

So Lizzy is in love with me? I guess that's probably something I knew. Deep in my brain. I recall the look on Maaz's face as he yelled at me for failing to save Lizzy. He probably knew it, too. But he definitely knows I'm not in love with Lizzy. Maybe that's why he hated me for so long. And yet, I'm the one who's going to be left alive with her after he dies out there.

That feels like a big responsibility.

I consider hooking in a line between just me and Maaz again. Asking him what he wants us to do. Asking him what he wants me to do. But I don't want to interrupt the last few minutes he has with her. It doesn't seem right, and I don't really need the extra confirmation.

"I promise, Anna," I say. "It's what Maaz would want me to do."

"Exactly," Anna says.

14.

LIZZY

I have never been more outraged in my life. Maaz is out here with Myles's stupid jetpack and his own stupid tank full of oxygen, and it is *completely* unfair that he is stronger than I am, because it means it doesn't matter how much I flail as he removes my jetpack and replaces it with Myles's. I am powerless to stop him.

I can still yell at him, though. And I do. I say things like, "why are you *doing* this!?" and "I could have died alone!" and "I don't want you here!" and "I'm not leaving you here to die alone either!"

At first, he ignores me, but after that last one, he starts talking back. Then it's chaos for a while as I keep ranting and he comes back with stuff like, "what were *you* thinking trying to save the pod instead of *yourself*?" and "you're *not* dying here!" and "I don't *care* what you want, I'm the one staying, *not you*!"

At that, I start crying—I guess maybe I'm just done with all this—and that turns out to be more effective than anything I've said. Maaz has that jetpack on me, but he stops yelling as soon as I start sobbing. Then he floats and puts his arm around me as best as he can with spacesuits, and now he's much calmer telling me it's okay, he knows what he's doing, and we're both going to be okay.

"Really, Lizzy," he says, and he has a look that is entirely too peaceful on his face as he says it. "I had a bad feeling before, but it's gone now. No one is going to die out here today."

"But what if you're wrong!?" I sob. "I can't *lose* you, Maaz."

He laughs. "At least it's not Myles you're losing."

That stings *bad*. Yes, I've had a big crush on Myles for most of my immortal life, but I've loved Maaz forever, and it never occurred to me to consider which one I'd rather lose. I wasn't supposed to lose either of them. Was that naïve? To think I could keep them both, but in different ways, for the rest of our immortal lives?

"Maaz, it would be just as bad to lose you as it would be to lose Myles," I tell my best and oldest friend. "I *love* you. You're like a—"

He holds up a gloved hand and closes his eyes. "Don't."

"But I—"

He opens his eyes again, and they're redder than I've ever seen. "Please, Lizzy. Don't say it. I have something to say first."

I'm afraid this is going to be our last conversation ever, so I stop trying to interrupt. Whatever he has to say, he needs to be allowed to say it.

It takes a while for him to work it out. Several minutes. Maybe five or so. I reminisce while he's forming whatever words he needs to say to me. I think of all the things Maaz and I got up to. I think of how long I've relied on Maaz to be a beacon for me. How long he's been the one person I could count on to cheer me up, to hold me up, to lift me up, no matter what. Even when Anna failed me. Even when *I* failed me.

He has been the light in my life.

He starts to talk.

"The thing is, I *don't* love you like family," he says. Whispers actually. Like this is a confession.

It makes my chest quiver.

He continues. "You're *everything* to me, Lizzy. I … I love you like if you die here, I might as well be dead myself. You're the person I'd follow across the *universe*. I *did* follow you across the universe. Because I'm in love with you. So if you die today, where will I be? But I know it's not the same for you, and that's okay. That's what makes it so that I'm the one whose life needs to be at stake here. Me. Not you. Do you understand?"

He has been holding onto me as tight as he can in a spacesuit, and he just said the most powerful thing *anyone* has ever said to me, and if we both make it back, we're going to have one hell of a conversation about this.

But I'm frozen on something else as he finishes his confession. His eyes. They're normal again. Golden bronze. Exactly the same shade as this whiskey we drink together sometimes.

Why didn't I know Maaz was in love with me?

Did I know?

"You are *not* dying today, understand?" he repeats. Then before I can do or say anything else, he unclips me from the water pod I fought so hard for and pushes us both away from it. I don't understand anything right now. Why is he pushing us away from the pod? I'm sure as hell not leaving him *now*, and we would be so much easier to find connected to the pod, and—

"I love you, Lizzy," he says, and he does something terrible. He uses the last jet fuel in his pack to push himself away from *me* and the pod and everything else. He flies away all at once and disappears from my sight.

"Where are you going?" I scream hysterically. I check my locator for him. One second I see him, and the next he's gone. Did he disable the locator? "Why did you *do* that?"

"I'm making sure you have no choice but to go back to the ship now," he says over the radio. "Don't waste the jetpack fuel. Go back to the Astronomia Nova. Go back to Myles. And just, don't forget me if you never see me again."

"No, Maaz!" I am in tears. So many tears.

"Please, Lizzy."

"Maaz, I love you, too." For the first time, I don't know exactly what I mean by that. Could I be in love with him? I didn't think so. But have I ever given him a real chance? What if the reason I never let myself fall for Maaz is that I needed him too much?

"I know," he says, and his voice is so gentle and understanding that I nearly break. "So I'm going to stop talking now. Because I need you to go back to the ship, and I don't want you wasting any more time. We can talk again when I know you're back on the ship."

There was a time when Maaz thought maybe he wasn't that smart. He probably thinks he's brilliant now. But I think he's totally stupid.

I go. Only because he gave me no other choice. And I am a mess by the time I reach the Astronomia Nova, where Myles is still waiting for me. He doesn't say anything to me when he sees me.

I look at my locater, and Maaz still isn't registering on it. "Maaz?" I say into the radio. "I'm back at the ship. You can talk to me now."

He doesn't answer.

"Why isn't he answering?" I say to Myles. "Has he been talking to you?"

Myles grimaces. "I think he wanted to make sure you got back inside the ship."

I practically drag Myles to the airlock, I'm going so fast.

Anna is waiting for me inside. She helps me out of my suit while I ask them about Maaz. What's the plan to save him? How are we going to do it? Who's going out to relieve him? Is he in contact with the command deck? Who's been talking to him?

My sister won't answer any of my questions. She just pulls me through the Astronomia Nova with Myles right behind me. A million people seem to be waiting for us. Crew members crowd the halls near the airlock. People cheer. Say my name. Say Myles's name. There are hands all over me— bumps and squeezes until they seem to realize I'm crying. Then it's gentler pats and hugs, but *still,* no one will tell me what we're doing for Maaz.

Anna and Myles usher me to the command deck, and there the scene is entirely somber.

"What's going on?" I ask breathlessly as soon as I see Commander Rowan. "Is Maaz talking again yet? What's our plan to bring him back in?"

Rowan can barely look at me. Anna has taken my hand and is squeezing it tight. Myles hasn't left my side yet either. I can feel his shoulder up against mine.

Maaz isn't talking to anyone over the radio.

Something happened. Something bad.

I break away from Anna and Myles and go for the radio myself. "Maaz?" I say into the com. "Maaz? Talk to us. How are you doing out there?"

There is no answer.

Commander Rowan looks like she's aged in the last eight hours, even though that's impossible for immortals our age. "Lizzy, we lost contact with Maaz shortly after you left him," she says.

"That's because he muted his radio," I explain. "He said he'd turn it back on after I got here." I speak into the radio again. "Maaz? I'm on board. You can unmute yourself and give us a status update. We're working on a plan."

Commander Rowan shakes her head. "Lizzy, you don't understand. We lost total contact. The locators can't find him at all. His vitals flatlined ten minutes ago."

"I think he turned his locator off," I say to Rowan. "But he's still out there. He couldn't have gone too far from the pod. He didn't have any jet fuel left."

"We detected two more interstellar winds," Commander Rowan says.

Myles actually hits something. One of the consoles. Hard. It makes a loud noise as what they're telling me hits me like a sack of bricks.

"So let's go after him," I say. It's even more urgent to me now. He's out there alone in dangerous conditions.

"We're not going after him," Commander Rowan says softly. "Without anything to track, we have no way of knowing which direction he might have gone, without the drones, we can't effectively search, and given the circumstances, we can't put anyone else at risk. We're still planning to recover the water pod. We'll search for him as soon as we have a drone for the task. But—"

"But we'll be searching for a body," I fill in, feeling totally hollowed out.

"Liz," I hear my sister say.

I was angry when Maaz came to rescue me from the pod. I'm even angrier now. Angry at him. Angry at Rowan. Angry at Yedda and Sterling and Xael. Angry at Anna.

I lash out at her first. "Why did you let him do it?" I say to my sister. "Why didn't *you* come for me instead?"

She looks like I slapped her. I don't even feel bad about it.

I turn on Commander Rowan next. "And why the hell isn't there a drone rover available? Who's overseeing that? Who let that ball drop?"

Myles comes over to me and puts his hand on my arm. He doesn't say anything, but I'm *furious* at him, and I think he knows it.

"And *you*," I say.

"I know," he says, right before I punch him hard, hitting just below his eye and making a mark spring up immediately.

He doesn't even flinch. No one does. No one says anything as I spend the next minutes saying all the things I shouldn't. Blaming everyone. Telling them all they should have let me *die*. I wasn't as selfish as any of them have been today. I didn't want to choose this. *Everyone* on this ship matters to someone. We *all* put ourselves in danger sometimes for the sake of someone else.

I was willing to go out there and die, and they should have let me.

And when I can't deal with the pain anymore, when I'm about to sink down onto the floor and sob, Myles puts his hand on my arm again. I catch Anna's eye. She is standing alone, her eyes glowing red and dripping with tears.

"Lizzy," she whispers.

"You *let* him do it," I hiss.

Myles tightens his grip on my arm. "We can pass that blame around. We all let him do it," he says. "Come on. Let's get out of here."

I am a mess as he leads me away from the command deck, and now word has spread that Maaz didn't make it, so this time it feels even *worse* as crew members I usually like and respect follow us through the ship, saying kind, horrible, genuine things that I don't want to hear right now.

"I'm so sorry, Lizzy."

"I'm so glad you're back, Lizzy."

"Is Maaz really gone?"

"I can't believe he's gone."

"We're going to miss him so much."

"He was a hero."

"We loved him so much."

We never loved him enough, I think.

"Everyone get the hell out of the way," Myles starts barking, and he sounds grouchy enough that people pay attention. That, at least, is a good thing.

Myles takes me to my private cabin, follows me in, and closes the door behind us. He maneuvers me like a puppet from the door to the edge of my bed. He locates a box of tissues, rubs my back, hands me tissues, and says nothing for the longest time while I cry and cry.

When I finally have no more tears left, he starts talking. "I'm sorry," he says. "And not just because it should have been me out there. I'm sorry I wasn't paying enough attention to you before. I'm sorry I never got to know Maaz better. I'm sorry I'm never going to be a good substitute for him. I'm sorry for all of us. None of us deserve this."

It's so honest it hurts.

I start crying again. "I didn't know him well enough,

either," I say through sniffs and sobs. "He was in love with me, and I had no idea. How did I not see that? How do you *miss* something like that?"

Myles responds softly. "Might not be as hard as you think. I may have missed something like that myself."

Oh, great. So he's realized I have this stupid crush on him. Or at least that I *had* a crush. For now, that crush is the smallest feeling in my body compared to everything I'm feeling about Maaz.

I hurt too much.

"Might have something to do with deciding you don't *want* to see it because you're too afraid of what will happen if you do." He leans my way, and his shoulder bumps mine. "In case you didn't know, by the way, you'd be a very easy person to love. If I wasn't so terrified of love. Maybe back before. When I was more like you."

"Maaz was like me from the beginning," I say, and that brutal truth makes the wound inside me worse. "And *he* was easy to love. Why didn't I let that in? Why did I refuse to even consider it? I was willing to consider just about everyone else. Why not him?"

Myles sighs. "Why does anyone ever die young? Why don't some people ever find love? Why do we do the worst things to the people who love us the most?"

I hate this.

I hate everything.

"I think I want to be alone," I tell Myles.

"I think I might have sort of promised Maaz I wouldn't leave you alone if something like this happened," he tells me.

"When?" I demand.

"When you weren't listening."

"Why?"

"I don't know. Something about honor between men who should never have been foes." He says that glibly, but then he grabs my hand. "And Lizzy, you've *always* been there for me when I can't think my way out of my own misery. What kind of friend would I be if I deserted you the one time your eyes turn red?"

"My eyes are red?" I rub them as if I can make it go away that way. I don't know the last time my eyes turned red. It hardly ever happens to me. "What do they look like?"

"Like you just lost the love of your life," Myles says. "But you're going to be okay. Probably not tomorrow. Or the next day. But someday you're going to wake up, and it won't hurt so bad."

"How do you know that? You seem to still wake up hurting pretty bad." It's cruel, but I had a shitty day, and Myles was part of it.

He flinches. "It's different for me. Sometimes, I feel like if I stop hurting, I'll lose the last piece of Stella I was hanging onto. And I'll have to try again, you know? Possibly let myself get hurt again. And I don't think I could handle that. But you're Lizzy Dupree. You have an infinite capacity for love, and that means you have an infinite capacity for loss, too. This is what you're good at."

"I don't feel like I'm good at any of that," I tell him.

"You're wrong," he says.

15.

ANNA

Lizzy is the one person I love more than anything in the universe, so when I found out she had gone off with Myles to fix some leak in one of the water pods, I was irate.

What was she *thinking?* There are a hundred people on board our ship, and we are all trained to do pretty much everything. I was sure she'd be better than *Myles* at finding the leak and repairing it, but that doesn't mean someone *else* couldn't have done it. Janis has smaller fingers. Kenton is our lead engineer. He knows how everything works.

Foster Hinks was the one who woke me up to tell me Lizzy had gone out into space again, and I shared my rant about how stupid it was as we rushed together from the cabins to the command deck.

"Sure, Anna, but Janis isn't a fixer, and Kenton freezes up when things go wrong," Foster said at the time. "And Lizzy is out there with Myles. Logically, it was the best choice."

I've never understood Lizzy's thing with Myles. She has nothing in common with him. She thinks he's smart, kind, good-looking, and deeply sensitive, but really, are those bars that high? Especially for someone amazing like her? He's also morose. He has a dry sense of humor. He's always itching to sacrifice himself for the greater good, and not because he wants to help the greater good, but because that would be a great excuse to get out of the rest of eternity.

He's selfish, like *me*, not her, and that's not good enough for Lizzy. The universe is a cruel place, and most of the humans living in it are barely keeping up their side of the bargain. Lizzy is the only truly good human in the universe. And anyway, I always thought that if she wanted love, she ought to get over her Myles fantasy and look at the real, uncomplicated choice standing right in front of her.

Now Maaz is gone, though. Gone gone. And it's been three hours since Lizzy locked herself away with Myles in her cabin, and it's the strangest thing for me. For the very first time, I think maybe she does need Myles right now. Not because *he's* ever going to love her right. Not because she needs pity sex or something. But because Myles understands something I don't think Lizzy has ever felt before: pure, hot *anger* at someone you love. The kind you feel when they do something that denies you the privilege of their company for the rest of your life.

I understand that feeling myself, but I wouldn't know how to help Lizzy. How could I? I *still* haven't forgiven our mother for dying. Or for ever loving our father to begin with. What a stupid mistake. Myles, on the other hand, forgave the dead girl he's still in love with hundreds of years ago.

Foster sits up with me while we wait for Lizzy and Myles to emerge from a pain comma. We don't know how long that will take. Maybe a few hours. Maybe a whole eight-hour sleep period. Maybe days. It'll happen sometime, though, and I figure that when it does, they'll need to eat something.

So Foster and I are in the kitchen, and I'm stress-baking space cookies. Not exactly something that requires finesse, but they'll serve as solid comfort food when Lizzy's appetite returns. And I need this right now.

"She was always like this," I tell Foster while I'm mixing cookie dough.

"Always heroic and unwilling to let someone she cares about risk their life for her?" Foster says.

I snort. "Always stupid and impulsive. She used to go to these crazy parties. Get drunk with strangers. Come home in the morning. I don't think she ever had a death wish, though. She thought she was invincible. Maaz has been watching for her to fly too close to the sun forever."

Foster, our head physician, is insightful about humans but not too tied to them. "Don't forget that we're immortals, Anna," he says. "No one on this ship is physiologically older than thirty or so. We may have the wisdom of a thousand years, but we're still prone to making rash decisions we wouldn't make if we were physiologically older. We're supposed to feel a little invincible."

I grunt. "But we're *not*."

Foster sighs. "No, we're not."

I think about Maaz, though, and the look on his face when he told us he was going out there as backup for Lizzy and Myles. He knew something was going to happen. I'm sure of it. He always knew when Lizzy needed him because he always loved her better than anyone else in the world. Probably even better than me. In that sense, he was invincible for us.

I'm going to do the best I can to honor the last promise I made Maaz: to stay with my sister for as long as I can. No one else can leave her like that. But I'm afraid. I'm not a reliable sister. What happens when I mess up? Will Lizzy be okay?

"Do the cookies need *that* many chocolate chips?" Foster says. I'm dumping the chocolate in and not thinking about what I'm doing, and there's going to be more chocolate than batter now. He smirks while I start scooping chocolate chips back into the container. "So, there *is* such a thing as too much chocolate?"

I put all those chocolate chips right back into the cookie batter. "No," I say. "Not for Lizzy, there's not."

Foster plucks a few chips out with his fingers and eats them. "I don't know anyone who does life better than Lizzy Dupree," he says. "Maaz was close, though. I can't believe we just lost him. But he knew what he was doing heading out there, didn't he? Knew how much we need Lizzy."

Maaz's face flashes through my mind one more time. Always calm. Always positive. *Always* there for Lizzy.

A tear slides down my face.

"It's okay to feel sad," Foster says. "You just lost someone who was probably like a brother to you." He pats my hand and doesn't say anything for a while, but at some point, he says, "Wonder if we'll ever find his body?"

I shiver at the thought of Maaz frozen and out of oxygen drifting forever through space, but the thought of finding him is even worse. That, I think, would destroy Lizzy.

"Hopefully, never," I say.

EPILOGUE
CHRISTIAN GODRIC

3442 CE Eden Immortality Spacecraft

"Why does love so often lead to unfathomable sacrifice? Why are we willing to give up *so much* for such a dangerous emotion? At what point does love become the enemy itself?"

I am pondering, as I often do, to a captive audience. This audience isn't my usual, though. This is a human we picked up a few days ago. The guy blew right into our ship like the meeting was pre-ordained, and I am fascinated by this auspicious event. He is the first human I've spoken to in over a millennia whose eyes weren't permanently reddened by the Immortality Virus. And yet, he appears to be immortal himself. I lean toward him, so I can really get a good look at those eyes. They're yellow—rare for humans generally, rarer for immortals—and there's a perpetual flame of fury raging in them right now. I don't think he likes us much.

Maybe it's the restraints. I made them painfully tight. That's how Mila likes it done.

"Am I *wrong* that your recent near-death predicament had something to do with a doomed love?" I lower my voice because I actually think I might want him to like me, and a soothing tone can help with these things. "I know something about being doomed."

"I bet you do," the man says, staring straight back at me in defiance as if to point out that *my* eyes are going to be red for the rest of my eternal life.

It's not my best feature, I'll admit, but if he's trying to taunt me, his taunts need some work. I am not that easy to goad. "There, now, there's no need to be nasty. You're going to be my guest for some time. Why don't you at least tell me where you came from? You were traveling with other humans, weren't you? From Earth?"

He doesn't answer, so that's a yes.

"And you seem to know who we are, but we don't know *you*. That must mean your ship launched quite a bit after ours. Maybe hundreds of years later. So you're a visitor from the future—" I pause and consider the scowl on his face "—but is the future friendly or—" he averts his eyes "are you my enemy?"

He makes eye contact again. "Are you *mine*?"

He's got some spunk. When we found this man, he was on the brink of death. Nearly out of oxygen. Suffering from hypothermia. Jet propulsion unit completely out of fuel.

The crew wanted to throw him back into space and let him die. We're always short on resources. We don't need one more mouth to breathe our oxygen and eat our food. And he had a tracking device on his suit, but he'd disabled it, so it didn't seem wrong to believe that he'd gone to a lot of trouble to die alone out there.

But the crew can be a bit short-sighted. When a universe as big as this one drops a human who might have useful information about the *future* right in front of your nose, you do not let him die. You pick him up, take him in, and squeeze him until you've juiced all that information right out.

"Well, *are* you my enemy?" he says. As if he's in control of this interrogation.

"*I* am Christian Godric," I tell him. "I am the second in command of a spacecraft the size of a small village heading to a planet with a plan to conquer, defeat, and dominate. I am not afraid to use, manipulate, hurt, or kill anyone I need to achieve my goals."

"Sounds like you're a real nice guy," the prisoner says.

I choose to loosen the restraints on his wrists. For now.

"But I have always *preferred* civility. If you're smart, you and I will be friends."

"You're an IV-933 immortal," the prisoner says. "By nature, you're willing to hurt and kill your friends. You can't help it."

I shrug. "Well, that seems to let me off the hook rather easy, doesn't it? But luckily for you, I'm smarter and more strategic than most immortals."

"So you're saying if I work with you, you won't stab me in the back?" he says. "Even if you're in a bad mood? Because *I've* never met an IV-933 immortal who could pull that off."

"Do you know many IV-933 immortals?" I ask.

"I've known a few," he says.

Hmm. Well. Maybe.

"Look, all I'm suggesting for now is we go tit-for-tat," I explain to the skeptic. "We are in an on-going prisoner's dilemma game. You show me I can trust you, and I'll show you that you can trust me, and repeat."

I'm going to give him some time to mull that over. A few days. Or a week. For the inconvenience he's causing me. But I tack on a useful disclaimer as I leave the cabin: "Oh, but I can never guarantee what I'll do if I'm in a bad mood. I pushed my best friend out of an airlock once. Happens when you're immortal."

I hear a harsh breath from the prisoner as I walk out, and I'm pleased with that. He'll have plenty to think about while he's in there, and if he comes to the right conclusions, maybe we'll decide to feed him.

One of my current lackeys is waiting for me outside the door with that nervous-but-not-quite-peeing-their-pants look people tend to get when they have bad news to tell me.

I sigh. "What is it?"

"There was a fight this morning on level two, Lord Godric," the lackey says. "We're low on water, and someone's been using three times as much as they're allowed."

Ahh. I happen to know what caused *that*. Mila has been taking rather long showers recently. Guess we'll have to decide if we're going to keep that our dirty little secret or tell them the empress requires additional water. I'd prefer the first, but she'll probably want the second. She's a bit of an exhibitionist sometimes. Thinks demanding special rights solidifies her power, and power is the only thing that satisfies her.

It's beautiful, I think. Her use of all that power. With every act, she becomes more corrupt, and I fall further into her snare. We weren't always this way. Not exactly. But she can't help who she's become, and I can't help but follow her down this road.

Why does love so often lead to unfathomable sacrifice? I, frankly, don't even like to admit that I've ever been in love, but I *am* certain that one day, the love that so ensnares me is going to lead me to a terrible and gut-wrenching demise, probably involving the loss of all that I still care about.

It is not going to be a happily ever after.

But who wants happily ever after anyway? That sounds boring as hell. If I ever get to a place in life where I'm truly, really happy, I shall give Mila permission to poison me. Luckily, we're not there yet. This story is far from over.

The End. (For now.)

THE STORY CONTINUES IN

THE IMMORTAL MISTAKES BOOK THREE

SANDRA L. VASHER

And find out what happens to your favorite immortals thousands of years later on Kepler in Sandra L. Vasher's

THE MORTAL HERITANCE

BOOK ONE
SISTERS OF THE PERILOUS HEART
MAY 2020

ACKNOWLEDGMENTS

I self-publish my books under my own independent publishing house, Mortal Ink Press, LLC. I use a number of resources as an indie publisher, including Scrivener, FlatIcon, FreePik, Adobe InDesign, Calibre, Affinity Designer, Grammarly, Shutterstock, and so on. My cover was designed by Danielle Doolittle at DoElle Designs. Danielle is great, and I highly recommend her! I write locally with the Raleigh Pubwriters and virtually with Word Stitch Write Ins. Look either of these groups up online, and you can write with me, too.

BOOKS BY SANDRA L. VASHER

The Immortal Mistakes
Stella Rose Gold for Eternity
Lizzy Dupree and the Thousand-Year Crush
Mila Hildebrand is Forever Not Yours

The Mortal Heritance
Sisters of the Perilous Heart
Kingdoms of the Frozen Dead (January 2021)

ABOUT THE AUTHOR

Sandra L. Vasher is an indie writer, recovering lawyer, dreamer, consultant, blogger, serial entrepreneur, and mommy of very spoiled dog. She enjoys long drives in fall weather, do-it-yourself projects, animated movies and cartoons, fanfiction, red wine, traveling everywhere, and baking sweet and savory treats. She can often be found trying not to hunch over her computer at her favorite coffee shops in Raleigh, North Carolina. Follow her online at sandyvasher.com.